I0538154

Mark McKnight: Author, Adventurer, Youth Worker, Saw Doctor, Snake Oil Salesman, Photographer, Armchair Theologian, Bass Player in Christian Death Metal Band 'Thrash! Amen'

This isn't the first thing he's written. But you're a smart person – you know how to use Google. If you want him, he's probably on Facebook right now. Oh, and you can always follow @irishmarko

500: A Collection Of Slightly Longer Stories
is his eighth printed work.

Forthcoming & already available titles
By Mark McKnight

Msimulizi: Stories For Mwangaza (2004)
Msimulizi 2: The Green Dragon (2005)
Msumulizi 3: Get Out Of My House! (2009)

The Village At The End Of The World (2006)
More Village At The End Of The World Stories (2009)
The Village At The Other End Of The World (2012)
The End Of The World At The Village At The End Of The World (2013)
The Book Of Secrets (2014)

On The Road (2005)
Christian Men Are W*nkers (2012)

500: A Collection Of Very Short Stories (2005)

For more copies of this book, good luck in finding them because there will probably only ever be a couple of copies printed – it's a fairly niche market. For copies of any of the other books listed above, talk to Mark first, because he has a couple of boxes full of books that he might be willing to give away without any money needing to change hands. Or buy them on Kindle – that seems to be what all the cool kids are doing these days.

You can also visit babymosquito.com but there's essentially nothing there for you to look at.

The profits of this book will not go towards philanthropy because it will, quite frankly, be a miracle if it even breaks even. And I lost a lot of money betting on a horse!

501:

A Collection Of
Slightly Longer Stories

Mark McKnight

Baby Mosquito Books

Acknowledgements

Last Summer, I had my heart broken by a beautiful young lady from South Wales. Seven of stories towards the end of the book are about everything that happened and how I turned from being a happy-go-lucky youth worker to a miserable, lonely old man. For a while! It still hurts, and I wish I knew and understood what exactly happened.

But you have to continue living. So my thanks to the Welsh for sending that particular woman into my life to give me the inspiration to finish the book.

I hold no ill-feeling towards the Welsh race in general.

Copyright © 2006-2011 by Mark McKnight

First published in 2012 by Baby Mosquito Books

The right of Mark McKnight to be identified as the Author of the Work has been asserted by him in accordance with the Copyright, Designs and Patents Act 1988.

ISBN 978-1-905691-09-8

This book has been typeset in Sanford, **Georgia** and **Verdana**

Printed and bound in Great Britain by Lightning Source Inc, Milton Keynes

Mark McKnight
189 Pendleton Road
Darlington
DL1 2EP
ENGLAND

http://www.babymosquito.com
mark@babymosquito.com

Not for Pete.
Thank God!

501:

A Collection Of
Slightly Longer Stories

Mark McKnight

Table of Contents

Prologue..11
Fearless & Insecure..12
Dishonourable Intentions...............................14
Shit Hole!...16
Just A Girl I Used To Know.............................18
Outside Looking In...20
Four In The Morning.......................................22
Blood, Sweat & Tears......................................24
A Tale Of Two Hotels 26
The Great Hair Experiment Of 2005...............28
Adolescence..30
Dear Daphne...32
Dangling Feet..34
Home...36
Rock Climber...38
Warriors...40
Rock Star..42
Thirteen...44
Hung. Over..46
Ears...48
Belgium!...50
Found A Frog...52
Magneto...54
Stud Of The Year...56
Internet Dating..58
The Brush Off..60
Your Smile Lights Up My Life...........................62
Happily Unhappily Single.................................64
Money..66
Blind Date From Hell......................................68
Break In..70
Do You Know What It Means?...........................72
Burns Night...74
Awkward...76
Chosen...78

Waiting...80
Royal Wedding...82
Ridiculous Vegetable Chopping Injury.....................84
Plus One...86
Losers...88
Emily Williams Posted On Your Wall.......................90
Lottery...94
Best Man...96
Things I Have Done To Impress A Girl.....................98
Lifelong Ambition..100
Silence..102
Home 2..104
Emotional Vacuum 106
If...108
Rock Music...110
Lonely...112
Hope...114
Power..116
The Meeting...118

Prologue

The idea of the 500 word word story began as an experiment in succinct storytelling – was it possible to tell a complete story in just 500 words. And after filling up a book with them, the answer came back as a very clear and resounding, "Maybe, maybe not!"

501 seemed to morph into a strange kind of autobiographical work of semi-fiction. Truth often turned out to be stranger than fiction, like the time I came home to find a burglar in my house.

It's been a tough year and lots of the later stories document some of the stuff I've had to struggle through emotionally. I abandoned my journal for a while in favour of 501 word stories as a kind of catharsis for fear and loneliness.

These stories represent pain, anger, disappointment and grief. There's some flights of fancy in here too – one or two based on reality with a very big 'what-if' and a couple of pure pieces of fiction. The problem with an over active imagination is that it tends to wander at will.

Fearless & Insecure

By Mark McKnight

I am fearless.

I am insecure.

The place where I grew up has many dangers. There is no easy life. There is no softly, softly approach. I will fight you any time, any where, any how. Just name the day and the place. I have destroyed tougher men than you. Where I come from, we don't worry so much about the police. If you want to steal from me, better make sure you can run. Fast. And don't ever show your face in this town again. You talk a good game but I will break your legs one by one if you ever touch me again. I'll give you one shot for free. Then we start. Little boy, you don't know what you're getting yourself in for. Okay now, you've had your say. Made yourself look like a real hard man in front of your mates. Now let me have my say. Listen to my accent. Where do you think I'm from? Do you really want to get into this with an Irishman?

I'm lonely. I want to tell you the truth – what I think about you but I'm afraid that it will destroy our friendship. I don't have many friends. What is that guy thinking about me – I tried to help him but I can see from the look in his eyes that he doesn't care. I know, I know – some people say nice things about me but I can give out meaningless platitudes just the same as the next guy. I wish I was more confident. I wish I was better looking. I wish I had a better body. I wish I had more money. I wish I was settled down. I wish I had a wife and kids of my own. I wish. I wish. I wish.

Hey, mind your own business. You ain't no kid of mine. What gives you the right to come in here and treat me like that? Boy, you're going to look pretty funny picking up your teeth with broken fingers. How dare you. After all that I've done for you. Come here. Yeah, I'll show you what I mean right now. [Shakes fists threateningly] You want a piece of me? Come on you punk. I ain't scared of you. Yeah, you *better* run. You can run, but I have a long memory. I ain't going to forget about you.

Five years. Shit! There's a curse on me – I'm sure of it. Someone up there doesn't like me. Five years, and what have I got to show for it? Not much – just a list of broken relationships, mediocre triumphs and bad attitudes. I give and I give and I give and I give. And with every piece that I give away, I lose something of myself. I am incomplete. The more I give the more incomplete I become. Who can love an incomplete man. Who can befriend someone who is not all there? Who? Who? Who? Who?

I am fearless.

I am insecure.

Gaba, 6th September 2006

Dishonourable Intentions

By Mark McKnight

I'm scared. Not the kind of fear that caused us to hide behind the sofa during episodes of Doctor Who while we were children. The kind of grown up fear that causes a deep rumbling in the pit of your stomach. The kind of grown up fear that causes you to wake in the night in a cold sweat, convinced of imminent doom. Yet this fear is not for my own safety or well being. I gave up on that long ago for I now have greater things to worry about than my own comfort.

My fear is for you: the daughter that I have not yet fathered. I have seen it many times before: in my dreams, in my own life and in the eyes of the girls who chance to pass me in the street. I know that look. I have seen the way they talk to the boys. They flick their hair, flutter their eyelashes and exude their sultry teenage femininity. They are everything that the boys are not. I know how much they love to talk to these boys. I know how much they crave the attention. I think I know how it feels to look in the eyes of a handsome boy.

But I also know what those boys think. I see how they playfully grab your hands. I see how they enjoy the hugs that you so gracefully bestow on both arrival and departure. I know how much they crave your attention for you are everything they are not. You are soft and curvaceous. You smell so sweet. You are attractive in every sense of the word. I know because I was once a teenager. I know beyond a shadow of a doubt how it feels to look in the eyes of a beautiful girl and have her look deeply into my own.

Just one look, one passionate embrace is all that is needed to begin the slippery downhill slope to ruin. To pregnancy. Or worse. Because in spite of all best laid plans, a man thinks not with his brain but rather with an organ much more base. Honourable intentions of the mind are soon replaced with the dishonourable intentions of a steamy Saturday afternoon in an empty house with an over-stuffed sofa. The same sofa that we hid behind as children during old episodes of Doctor Who. Now, as they rerun the old series, that sofa is exploited in a singularly different fashion.

Like a dog on heat, the hormones course through a boys' veins. He cannot change what he cannot control. These urges are to him as complex as they are to you. And just like a dog on heat, the only way (and even then of only limited success) is release or flagellation. A stick would suffice for an animal but these are sons not dogs. Yet neither option provides release for long. These young men, they are as they are – created in the image of God. Sons. Not. Dogs.

Gaba, 5th September 2006

Shit Hole!

By Mark McKnight

You and I, we go back a long way. We've been to some pretty places together. You have such a sweet spirit. I feel privileged to count you among my friends.

And now, five years after we first met, I come to visit your house. This shit hole in the middle of a shit village in a shit town.

Bad things have happened here. These fields are the killing fields. Bad things. Good pineapples.

As we sit on a coarsely made wooden bench, watching your grandmother, your aunt and your sister scratching around in the dirt for precious little food, what am I supposed to think. I am not your father. You are not my responsibility. You are someone else's daughter. And yet, am I partly responsible for this.

Mud walls, a tin roof. This house will not stand for so much longer. There are termites eating the wooden frame. The question is not if but when it will fall.

Inside men sit and talk, laugh and play their games. Outside, women and children dig for that is their lot.

"Uncle, you see how village life is tough." That is what you say. For my part, I can only nod and agree.

"Uncle, you see how life is tough for women." That is what you say. For my part, I can only nod and agree.

Children come to see this ghost white face that seems so out of place sitting below a tree that also will not remain erect for much longer – the wood is more useful as charcoal than as a tree. They creep up behind me, daring each other to get closer and closer. Unsure of how they should respond to this stranger in their midst.

And all too soon it is time to depart. Make my excuses. Avoid eating your food because God knows you need it more than I do. Avoid eating your food because, in all honesty, I can't stand to eat it. Most days, neither can you but, you see, I have a choice.

I can get on a plane this afternoon and return to the land of plenty should I so choose. I can buy some pineapples on the way home, get a Coke and forget what I have seen. You don't have that luxury.

I can see it in your eyes as I climb on the back of the motorbike. That half crazed mix of fear, desperation and resignation to your lot in life. You know that it might get better. You know that it might not.

And yet, there is some hope in your eyes. You are a smart

girl. You go to school. You study. You are the best in your class. Maybe you can escape from this place, make something of yourself.

As I leave, I thrust some money in your hand. The equivalent of a couple of quid. A Big Mac. A cup of coffee. A pint of Guinness. A difference between life and death in this shit hole.

Gaba, 6th September 2006

Just A Girl I Used To Know

By Mark McKnight

You see that girl sitting on the bench over there? Yeah, the blonde one. I used to be in love with that girl. It wasn't just puppy love either. I was really in love with her. Our souls actually connected. We spent every free moment together. Our love was chaste through no fault of mine or hers – just the way circumstances conspired against us.

You see that black girl over there? Yeah, the one with the short hair. She used to be in love with me. Had I not been so blind, I might have seen it before it was too late. Looking back, I can see that she was putting out all the right signals and I was mostly ignoring them.

You see that girl over there, driving past in her car? Yeah, the one in the pink dress. I could have been in love with her. I suppose it was all about time – she had too much of it and I didn't have enough. She was ready to settle down, I wasn't. I guess it wasn't meant to be.

You see that girl over there, the strange looking one? Yeah, the one with ginger hair. She broke my heart once. I met her and courted her but, just like everyone warned me, she turned out to have some serious issues. Two times, a year apart she came a-knocking. Things could have worked out except for the blonde girl on the bench – she was her best friend!

You see that girl with the puppy over there? Yeah, the one with the brown hair. She stalked me briefly a couple of years ago. I know, it sounds like I'm making it up but this is the truth. She sent me some rather revealing pictures of herself. I think she got bored of me ignoring her so she just went on to stalk someone else. My loss is someone else's gain!

You see that girl with the red sweater over there? Yeah, the one with braids. I should have kissed her years ago but I was too scared back then. Matter of fact, I reckon I'm too scared now. She had some commitments too – kissing a white man might have been a big deal for her pledge sisters.

You see that girl over there in the jeans? Yeah, the one with the curly hair. She and I dated for a while. Then I found out she was my cousin. After that, she dated my best friend. Then my best friend dated my sister. That was a real mess, my friend!

You see that girl over there with the long hair? Yeah, the one that's smiling and waving. She and I dated and broke up and then dated and broke up. Oh, and then we got married. She's my wife now. We have a little girl.

You see that girl over there with the flute case in her hands. Yeah, the pretty one. Nah, she's just a girl I used to know.

Gaba, 18th September 2006

Outside Looking In

By Mark McKnight

Here I stand, on the outside looking in. Through frosted, dirty glass I can see the warm glow: the embers of a dying fire and the faded aura of a party of friends recently split asunder, merely for the evening. The doors open and spill happy, contented and slightly drunken bodies into the bitterly cold January night: their hot breath steaming, their bodies wrapped against the chill.

As they enter their assorted conveyances (cars, vans, trucks), I still stand, on the outside looking in. Now their hot breath and hot bodies steam the frigid glass of their windows, obscuring my view that I can see only vague, dark shadows first talking, then moving and then talking again.

They depart and I am once again left alone. I still stand on the outside looking in. This time through the same grimy pane of glass. Now I see you, sitting all alone, unaware of the pair of eyes that watch your every move.

Yet despite your loneliness, you will never invite me in. It is my lot: I must remain here in the biting cold of another Irish winter. Like the shape of an X, our lives intersected all too briefly and since then we have separated. The relentless speed and motion of life came between us. I am no longer the man you once thought me to be. I am no longer the one in whom you sought and found refuge. I am no longer the one who nursed you through sickness, held your hand through trials.

Where has that fleeting moment gone? It is a mere memory: a vapour in the wind.

And so I stand, on the outside looking in. Maybe I will try a different window tomorrow. Look through the looking glass of someone else's soul. Maybe they will have the courage to invite me in. To sup with me. To share their life with me. To trust me. To love me.

At a new window I stand, on the outside looking in. Through a clean and freshly polished pane I can see new people, new things, new places. But the more I look, the more the glass begins to taint. Before I realise what has happened, my own grubby fingerprints cover the glass. It is then that I realise. It's not that you didn't want to see me through your window. My own failings made the glass so dingy and soiled that you couldn't see me any more. For that I am truly sorry.

I return to your window and begin polishing. My shirt sleeve is the best I can manage. For a brief moment, I see your face in crystal clarity, gazing through the glass. But as I polish, the glass continues to smudge and you are gone once more.

Here I stand, on the outside looking in. Your life is no longer my responsibility and mine is not longer yours. Fare well and try to make sure you always stay within rather than without the window.

Gaba, 27th September 2006

Four In The Morning

By Mark McKnight

I lie here at four in the morning with a thousand thoughts swimming round the whirlpool of my mind, each one of them chasing sleep away. The Guinness in my stomach which usually aids my slumbers is tonight aiding my troubled mind to pursue oblivion from within my grasp. Occasionally, maybe once every half hour it seems that dreams are within my grasp but as my mind realises the precariousness of the situation, I feel the sleep lose substance and trickle through my tightly clenched fist like dry sand.

And so I am resigned to lie here, worrying, fretting, panicking, crying, shouting, tossing, turning, sweating. The fury rises in my psyche. The more angry I become, the less I am able to sleep.

I read a book. Maybe that will hasten the passage of time to bring me closer to the moment of quiet. Yet the text, regardless of its interest in daylight hours, becomes impossible to stop reading. I can no longer fold the page, close the cover and fall asleep. I have to know the rest of the story tonight: I can wait no longer.

I use every trick in the book. I count sheep. I pretend I am in a boring meeting. I use relaxation exercises. Everything I can think of is met with abject failure for I still lie here awake, wondering if I will ever sleep again.

I arise, to find some solace, maybe some food will salve my harried mind. I eat and though it curbs the pangs of hunger, it does nothing to bring sleep to my alert eyes or my weary body.

For therein lies the duality of it. My body is tired. Dog tired. Yet my mind is alert. I think of so many different things: the past, the present and the future all at once. As I listen to the clock ticking, so oddly loud at this time of the night, and every stirring in this old house grates on my nerves, it comes from behind, ever so gradually. Like a black mist, sleep comes from behind without warning. Before I even realise it, I am asleep. I am still. There is nothing.

Yet just before my eyes finally close, there comes that brief moment of supreme clarity. That moment that only comes at four in the morning. As the morning slowly begins to break and the dawn chorus begins its first bars, I resign myself to the fact that sleep will not come this night. I have failed in my attempts. Might as well give up trying to dream as a lost cause.

And just as that thought becomes fully formed in my mind,

the black mist washes over me. I am still. Though this will be a short slumber, it is the drug that my body has been so desperately craving for many hours. Like an addict, my body and mind drink in the precious slumber, the respite that will enable me to face another day. I am still.

Gaba, 29th November 2006

Blood, Sweat & Tears

By Mark McKnight

A couple of pints of blood. Several gallons of sweat. Just one very small tear. That is what I have invested in you. That is what my body has sacrificed for you. But that is not all. Several thousand dollars of my own (and some not my own). About two years of my life. That's ten percent: my tithe.

I have sat in hospital waiting rooms, held your hand in the dentist's chair, cajoled you into taking the medicine that would make you well, driven you thousands of miles across deserts, swamps, jungles and cities. We were together on the single best day and the single worst day of my life. We were together on a hundred and one mediocre days in between.

You have watched my romances wax and wane. You have seen my anger, my bitterness, my fear, my hatred. You have seen me when I'm happy, lonely, tired, hungry, playful, furious, bored, busy and stressed. And I you.

You are a part of me and I am a part of you.

Yet even still, I fear that maybe I have taught you too well. There was a time when I was there for you 24 hours every day and seven days every week. I stayed up late many a night nursing you back to health, or just when you couldn't sleep. I rose from my slumber many a morning to get breakfast or just to make sure you had slept well. In fact, now that I think about it, let me add to my list the hours of lost sleep I have given you for I will not get those back.

Yet it seems that these days, I don't feature so highly in your list of important things. You see me in the street and say a quick hello and that is it. Sometimes I am treated with scorn and disdain – I am not cool enough for your friends. For that I am truly sorry but I am not the one who has changed. You are the one who has grown. You are the one who no longer needs me. It never crosses your busy teenage mind that maybe some days I need you too.

Of course, sixteen is an awkward age – so insecure, so alone yet desperately seeking your own independence. Your place in the world. Your identity. And so I become a casualty to that same independence. I do not fit in with your world. I am from another place. That is the change from my investment. That is what is left over. A few dirty old coins that don't amount to much.

A couple of pints of blood, several gallons of sweat and just one very small tear in exchange for your life: confident, ambitious, fearless. That is what I have traded. May God bless you. My body has made sacrifices to make you more complete and for that I am glad. As for me, I would give it all again. It is my destiny.

Gaba, 5th-6th September 2006

A Tale Of Two Hotels

By Mark McKnight

The first hotel we stay at on our two day trip to Kigali is really only a hotel in name only. 'Hotel' is almost an anagram of what it really is: a brothel. That's not to say it's a dump or anything. It's actually an okay place, if you compare it to some of the dives we've stayed in. Like the hotel where they charged you by the hour instead of for the whole night in Masaka. Or the hotel where it cost more for a soda than for an entire night's accommodation, where we had to hide from the rebels because we were white.

So here we sit in our simple hotel room with two trash cans: one for trash, one for used condoms. We idly joke that this is so that they can recycle although here, it doesn't even bear thinking about. The television is old and idiosyncratic so we have to call the man who shows up with a screwdriver and a pair of pliers. Soon, we are watching programming that is either in French or so piss poor that it isn't worth watching anyway.

Our friend Dave isn't coping well with slumming it. He's used to the high life. We may in fact be his friends in low places. For dinner last night, we ate at the Hotel Intercontinental. THE best hotel in Rwanda. It's owned by the government. Dave suggests that we move house. More accurately, move hotel.

Despite our (admittedly weak) protestations, Dave prevails and so we board some bodas – the equivalent of a motorbike taxi service bound for luxury beyond Adam and I's wildest dreams. When we arrive, the rooms are considerably more expensive than we two missionaries had expected. Dave, however, is undaunted. He begins negotiation and soon we have secured a suite at the Hotel Intercontinental for less than half the advertised price.

The second hotel we stay at on our two day trip to Kigali is something beyond what we ever expected to experience. We visited here a couple of years ago, amazed at its opulence. Sumptuous sofas, a luxuriant swimming pool, live music and that was before we had even seen the bedrooms.

Room service was the start of it but the thing that we were most excited about was how clean it was. No matter the cleanliness of the hotel itself, they had hot water. My first hot shower in eight weeks (not my first shower in eight weeks I hasten to add). We were so clean it was beyond reason. And the snow-white bath robes were the crowning glory.

Yet even so, all good things must come to an end and the

following day we boarded the bus back home. Nine hours of if not hell then at the very least purgatory through the mountains of Rwanda and the arduous terrain of south west Uganda.

When we got back, Dave had had enough. He packed bags and left us to our cold showers and bare stone floor.

Gaba, 23rd October 2006

The Great Hair Experiment Of 2005

By Mark McKnight

I shall grow my hair. I may never cut it again. Long hair that I can
braid or plait or tie up in pigtails. Well, maybe not tie up in
pigtails. That would be a little...well...you know...
I'm getting sidetracked.
"I shall grow my hair." That was my resolution on Saturday
January 1st, 2005.
Little did I know then the extremes of emotion my flowing locks
would effect.

This solemn occasion needed a marker. A gesture to signify the
beginning of the Great Hair Experiment of 1987. With gravity, I
shaved my head with a straight razor. If this were to be the last
time I cropped my ill-coiffed tresses, I would do it in style.

The skin head faces several main problems. The first is that within
an hour or two, their noggin is essentially covered in velcro™.
Second, without hair to protect previously unprotected scalp,
sunburn is major inconvenience. But thirdly, and most exigent is
that when you have a skin head, you look like a skin head.

As the hair grows, gel, mousse and hair spray are your friends.
They keep a short head of hair neat and tidy giving style and
adding character.

The next stage is the killer. For well nigh on a year, nothing can
be done. The locks are too long to even approximate being tidy
and too short to actually do anything with them. Wearing a hat is
just about the best way to get around.

In due course, the great day arrives when you can tie your hair
back. This is a moment that must be celebrated. Finally you can
braid. You can plait. You can tie it up in pig tails. Well, maybe
not tie up in pigtails. That would be a little...well...you know...

I learned a lesson about women and talking when I had my hair
braided. The first time I went to get my hair braided, it took her
two hours. They concentrated, dealt with the job in hand and did
some excellent work. The corn rows weren't perfectly straight but
all in all it was a good job.
The second time went to get my hair braided, her sisters was

there. And three of her friends. Four and a half flipping hours of having my hair pulled. And the corn rows were all over the place. Not her best work. Not by a long shot.

When I got home, the more I looked at myself in the mirror, the more I hated it. I was so angry that after a week I took the braids out in our living room one night. That didn't make me feel any better so I got the clippers and shaved my head. That didn't make me feel better either so I got a razor and shaved it properly.

And so ended the Great Hair Experiment of 2005 after 18 months. Every now and then I think 'I shall grow my hair...'
Then I remember the last time.

Darlington, 3rd March 2009

Adolescence

By Mark McKnight

You need me.
I don't know how or why or what for. But you need me.
Truthfully, I didn't think it would happen this quickly. It's only
been six months. Only six months to wipe away everything that
came before. Replace it all with me. Me. Me? Me!
Seems like a poor choice. Me, that's only just getting away with it.
A short step from being exposed as a fraud and a phony. Bad
social skills, bad jokes, bad fashion, bad choices, bad relationships,
bad example.
But you need me.
Somehow I've been entrusted with the weighty task of
shepherding you through adolescence. Making you into a man.
Or a woman. It's a heavy burden. A responsibility almost too
much to bear. When I think about it, I want to run. Go back to a
rose-tinted era when all I had to do was push buttons.
So I don't think about it. I get my head down and do the best I
can. Talk my half baked ideas up so that others think they're
great. Play the numbers game. Dazzle my bosses with everything
that is supposedly happening.
But there's no fooling you. When I slip up, you see me. When
I'm not smart enough to keep my big mouth shut, you hear me.
When my life isn't marked with the grace and love and wisdom
and integrity that I want it to be, you're there; watching every
move and listening to every word.
And yet every time I hold my hands up to admit that I'm a bad
person, you accept me. Trusting EVERYTHING I say. You
question every other adult in your life. Parents. Teachers.
Authority in all its diverse forms from the school librarian to the
police officer. But you don't question me.
Because you need me.
The person who will never ever tell you that you aren't valuable.
The person who always speaks life, not death. Someone who just
knows when things aren't right. And who cares. Someone who's
there every hour of every day. Not to talk to every hour of every
day but just someone who's there. Just in case.
You know. You understand, whether you can articulate it or not.
I am the one who's meant to help you grow up. That's why it
hurts so much. There's no such thing as a replacement. It's
just...well...different.
Then I get to thinking about it again. Am I that person?

Introverted. Shy. Not good with people. Not good with crowds. Not good speaking in public. Nothing worth saying. Definitely nobody worth following. And yet here I am; a semi-reluctant tour guide through the snares and pitfalls of growing up. Painfully aware of the ever present dangers of a crumbling world. A world that I love so very much.

You couldn't pay me to be a teenager again. I wouldn't do it.

You need me.

I don't know how or why or what for.

But you need me.

I probably need you too.

Darlington, 25th February 2009

Dear Daphne

By Mark McKnight

Dear Daphne,
We used to talk and laugh and play and sing. You danced, I joked, you had fun, I told stories. But now those days are gone and forgotten. Those days passed and you forgot me. New friends, new people to talk to, new faces to see and love. Once I mourned the passing of those carefree days of Spring.
And now that Spring is here again after waxing and waning four more times, I'm left to ponder if I still care. I think about you now and then. But time plays strange tricks on the mind. The gut wrenching pain of leaving. The yearning to be reunited. All gone. Those days passed and I forgot you. New friends, new people to talk to, new faces to see and love.
But where and why is that bond we had? I made a difference to you, just as you made a difference to me. Didn't I?
You made me more than I was before. Better than I was before. More human. Your faith, your strength, your love, your life. It changed me. It changed all of us.
But where am I now? How did I end up here? Where is our family?
All we had was each other. No-one else to lean on. We were each other's rock. These days, it seems like we have a thousand people each to tell us who we are and how we should live our lives. With so many to people lean on, we don't need to lean so hard on one person. So now all is superficial. Like the outsiders we disdained before. Nobody knows us or loves us the way we once loved each other.
Maybe one day I will find that depth of humanity again. To love and be loved. To need and be needed. To live and help others live.
Until then, tell me where you are? How has life treated you? Did I really change your life the way you changed mine? I like to think that I gave you grace, love, wisdom, integrity. I'm frightened that I gave you impatience, immaturity, shoddy workmanship and a lack of the very things I wanted to teach you. Best case scenario, I didn't make your life any worse.
Maybe this year I'll come across you again. See you down the street as I buy some kicommando in the village. Or you'll be there buying some mandazi as I stock up on rolex. And it won't ever be like it was before. Because everyone else is still around.
Watching. Listening. Judging.

So when you see me on the street, just give me a nod. I'll know what it means. And when I see you by the lake I'll give you a wink. You'll know what it means.
Those days passed. You forgot me. I forgot you. For my part, I am truly sorry. Maybe one day you'll understand what happened. Maybe one day I'll understand too. I'll see you this Summer, sweetie.

Darlington, 10th February 2009

Dangling Feet

By Mark McKnight

We're sitting here on a cliff, with our feet dangling off the edge of the world. Not the real edge of the world, of course. That would simply be ridiculous. Rather, we sit with our feet dangling over the edge of our own little world. A world carefully crafted and cultivated. The leaves have fallen five times and five times have we journeyed the world together.

Three continents, three failed romances (one for you, two for me) and three near death experiences. It has at times been euphoric and at times painfully banal. We've both had diseases of public health significance and both recovered. We've shared journeys by plane, train, boat, car, motorcycle and one disastrous trip through East Africa on a bus. And a hundred other bus trips. Some have been filled with pleasure, watching Kenny Rogers music videos, eating sausages and drinking cold, cold soda. Others have been a trial to be endured, watching street kids sniff glue, refusing qat and drinking lukewarm soda.

And as we sit dangling our feet, it slowly dawns on both of us that the world we have created is not the solid ground on which we sit. Our world is what lies below. The gaping chasm and wispy low level clouds of a life less ordinary. All that is in our world is uncertainty, insecurity and the thin mask of self-deprecating humour.

A rustling in the grass behind us makes us both turn our heads. It is woman. Blonde. Beautiful. And as we look at each other, we realise the precariousness of our situation. This is no solid rock on which we sit. This is a precipice on which we are suspended over the long drop back into the lifestyle to which we have grown accustomed. Were we both to stand up, the weak rock would surely break and we, all three of us, would tumble into the oblivion of a life dedicated to bachelorhood.

Who will stand and follow this vision of loveliness. I have learned humility and self-sacrifice from you. It must be you, for I am not of worth. You are the one who must go and I am the one who must stay.

Yet as you stand and take your first few faltering steps onto ground that is marginally more solid, I can hear the ground on which I sit begin to shift. I have time only to bid you farewell and offer up a meaningless platitude that I probably don't mean anyway before the landslide begins.

My slow descent begins back to my previous life. As I fall, I can see the look on your face. You are happy. My sacrifice has been worthwhile. Before long, my slow drop will cease and I can begin my climb back to the top, to find some solid ground. To find myself. To find my other. For now, I am happy you are happy. I am joyful in your joy. Next time, I may not make the same sacrifice.

Gaba, 17th November 2006

Home

By Mark McKnight

It's been two cold, harsh winters in the wilderness of western Europe since I left. I tied all the loose ends together in a knot that I thought was secure. No unfinished business. Everything done and dusted. I was not going back. East Africa had no place for me and I had no place for it. And for the last two years I put it out of my mind. Pushed it to one side where I didn't need to think about it. Didn't need to deal with it. Ignored the pain that I still was carrying. Suppressed the thoughts and the things that reminded of you.

Africa, you hurt me. Badly.
I only figured it out a couple of days ago.

I left because you injured me so severely. Real pain. As I boarded the plane, I glanced over my shoulder and looked at an Africa that I no longer loved. The vast African plains that once held my heart no longer captivated me in the same way.

I'm not coming back here.
And then I reconsider. It seems too much like an ultimatum. Let's try something with less finality.
I'm not coming back here unless I bring my wife with me.

There's this part of me deep within, that I will probably never fully acknowledge while sober, that made this covenant. It thinks, 'If I never get married, I'll never need to go back.' And then it thinks, 'That might not be too bad.'

On the way back on the plane, I begin to think about home. I've questioned this concept for several years now, mostly because I don't have one. I thought it was Africa. That didn't happen. I really didn't want it to be Northern Ireland. I <u>don't</u> want to go back there. It would be like admitting defeat. I thought it could be England. But there was no job for me, so I moved. Then I got fired so I moved. Then I found a home but didn't have a job.

So now I've found a home in Darlington of all places. I was comfortable. Happy to potter through the next couple of years as a youth worker. Things were falling into place. A house. A car. Friends. A job. I take a vacation. Reconnect with some people from my past. And that's when it all falls apart again.

That knot that I thought was tied so securely has started to unravel. If it was one end come loose, I could ignore it. Forget I came here. Go back to the life that I thought worked. But there's so many ends that have come loose, I might be in serious trouble.

Africa, you hurt me. Badly.
And I have two choices. I can untangle everything and find out exactly where all these strings end up. Except that will mean confronting the pain. Or I can tie up the ends and go back to my life. But for how much longer will they stay tied up this time?

Camarillo CA, 12th April 2009
(Easter Sunday)

Rock Climber

By Mark McKnight

Three winters it's taken me to climb back up this cliff. At times the going was easy. At times I cursed the razor sharp rocks that often times drew blood from my hands and feet. Resting in an uncomfortable crevice in the rock, I look down and see the world that once was mine. But it is no longer my existence. For as I look up, I see the same cliff over which we dangled our feet so long ago.

You've changed. You're not a different person. You've just changed. It's almost as if you're...better. For you no longer stand on that cliff by yourself.

The problem is this: although my resting place isn't perfect, it works. I can hide here from the elements. Falling rocks can't hurt me. I'm protected. But to climb right to the top of the cliff where once we dangled our feet and where once I fell before will be nothing short of tortuous. I remember what the ground was like up there. I remember the struggle to reach it the first time.

I've come this far so although my body resists, my mind knows that this crevice is not home. Home is at the top where the soft green grass grows. Where the ground is unstable but maybe that's the point.

As I reach out for the first hand grip with scarred hands, I hear a familiar rustling in the grass at the top of the cliff. It is woman. Blonde. Beautiful. For a brief moment, a memory flits through my mind. This is a precipice on which I alone am suspended over the long drop back into the lifestyle to which I am no longer accustomed. Hanging from hand grips that may or may not support me and that I am ill-equipped to climb on.

Except it's different this time. The ground is firmer. Somehow, I know how to climb to the top, where to put my hands and feet. I have the strength to pull my frame up the rock face. And I realise that I am supported by both harness and rope. And there she is, on the other end of the rope.

I can feel the light fading around me and fast. I must reach the top before darkness envelopes the clifftop. The darkness contains past mistakes, Goliath In Hot pursuit across the rocks.

From my perspective, it is as much an accident as anything else that I reach the top, or the will of a grand overseeing designer. Is this fate? Is this destiny? As I embrace you, I feel the icy fingers that have followed me up the cliff pulling me back towards my previous responsibilities: unfinished business, unfinished people.

But this time, as I am pulled away from you back to the life I have chosen, where all I have tried to do is follow I realise that the harness is still attached. And I know this is not the end. This is only the beginning.

Darlington, 21st April 2009

Warriors

By Mark McKnight

Here we stand, shoulder to shoulder, ready. Outmanned and outgunned by a force feared by all, we the warriors stand as the protectors of our way of life. As boys we were taught to hunt, to fish and to farm. We were taught to handle a weapon should the need arise. In our youthful bravado, we ignored the warnings about what battle really meant. This moment of bitter anticipation, before the fray, turns boy into man. And occasionally man into boy.

The smell of fresh urine where grown men have pissed themselves in fear. Of vomit where the courageous have regurgitated. Of the faeces of men who could hold it in no longer and shit right there beside us.

Those smells will soon be replaced by something far worse: the dull metallic odour of blood. Blood from two cliques of humanity smeared across a battlefield for which neither side cares. And as the battle rages, that smell of death becomes a taste too. Maybe even my own blood. It's difficult to tell as the adrenaline races through my veins.

The eerie silence that hung over the field before the engagement soon gives way to the impassioned speeches of two generals. One for us, one for them. And that soon gives way to the war cries of two armies ready to bear down on one another. Every time it is the same. The fervent preacher of war concludes followed by complete calm that lasts for four seconds. Every time four seconds. Then a cry goes up somewhere in the ranks and everyone begins to shout and yell. Banging the tip of their sword against their shield. Sometimes, a man will break ranks and turn to run. Rarely will he leave the field for desertion of duty is a grave offence. He will return to his rank or he will die by the sword of his comrades. The noise is deafening and for one sweet moment, all of life makes sense.

It is that moment that defines us. That moment that gives us the right to our name. For we are warriors, standing shoulder to shoulder with our friends and brothers. As the war cry builds, our breathing gets deeper and slower. Something else takes over. And then, with no signal, the war cry goes silent. No drum is beaten, no bugle blown, no order from our superiors. Still for less than one second, we stop our shout. It lasts for such a short time but it feels like forever. This is the point of no return. No more talk, no more politics. This is battle.

And as we each one raise our swords in the air, the warriors charge, like an unstoppable wave on the ocean. Slowly at first, then gathering speed towards another wave from another army. To glory or to oblivion, only time will tell. As we run towards the enemy, our entire world is that battlefield. We may live to fight another day. We may not. We are warriors.

Darlington, 22nd-23rd April 2009

Rock Star

By Mark McKnight

Nervous energy has been building all day. This feeling never changes. All through sound check and dinner, the sensation builds. A heady, intoxicating mixture of fear and exhilaration. The closer we get to start time, the more skittish people become. Tempers begin to fray, patience wears thin. This is not the time to talk. This is the time to close into yourself and your own thoughts.

Flies up, phones off. The final check before we walk out onto the stage. The lights are dark and I am illuminated only by the emergency lights that cast a subdued glow on the stage. The audience know we are there but play a charade as if we are not – in an ideal world we would not be seen as we walk to our starting positions, one on a drum stool and the rest of us at each of three microphone stands. For about ten seconds, we each have our own little routine before the crowd will bay for us to entertain them.

Our singer adjusts. Fixes his microphone stand, presses some pedals with his left foot. Adjusts the microphone stand again. Tunes his guitar. Presses some more pedals with his other foot. Drummer boy prickles with nervous energy. His fingers twitch. His feet tap the ground. He wriggles on his stool to get comfortable. The keyboard player interlocks his fingers and cracks all of his knuckles at once then checks his pedal is in the right place.

I stand with my back to the audience, bass guitar hanging loosely at my side. The nerves in my fingers tingle. The butterflies in my stomach begin to rise. I close my eyes, tilt my head back and breathe deeply. The faint musty smell of sound equipment mixed with our lead singer's aftershave.

This all happens in the first five seconds. About five seconds in, the audience begin to get edgy when they realise we are essentially standing doing nothing. One person will holler or whistle or scream and before long the whole crowd has taken it up. And it builds...and builds...and builds...and builds.

For now, the entire gig is on me. I give the count for our first song. So for the next five seconds or so I keep my eyes half closed, look up at the lighting rig and get in the groove, finding the tempo. I don't know what the rest of the band do for the next five seconds.

By the time the audience has reached fever pitch, I'm

ready to start. I turn to the drummer, almost unseen in the half light of the pre-gig lighting and yell (for it is the only way to be heard) 1-2-3-4. I take the upbeat and the drummer joins the next bar. The lights burst colour: purple, yellow, blue, green. The rest of the band join in. The sound system pumps a million watts to a thousand expectant faces. I turn to face the audience. The rock star.

Darlington, 23rd April 2009

Thirteen

By Mark McKnight

To be thirteen again! Desperately trying to be accepted by your peers, gaining some independence from your parents and finding a niche in this world. Your own body changing in frightening ways that you don't fully understand. Discovering girls who jump up and down and scream at the slightest provocation and whose bodies are changing in exciting ways that you don't fully understand. Or discovering boys with suddenly deep voices and whose bodies really don't seem to be changing much at all that you can see. For the first time, it seems that your previously protective and controlling parents will let you out of their sight, at least for a little while. Finding those places where you aren't under the watchful eyes of an adult and working out for the first time how to relate to your peers. Finding out what is cool and what is not: music, clothes, hairstyles, shoes. Finding out if you're cool or if you're not. To have your life ahead of you, full of idealism, youthful vigour and an unshakeable conviction that you know everything. Everything!

But therein lies the inherent arbitrary nature of life as we know it. Now that I have some comprehension of how this world operates, I have rethought some of the decisions of the last twenty years. The painful conclusion is that when I was young enough to do anything I wanted, I couldn't grasp that I really could do anything I wanted. And now that I finally appreciate the weight of this, I'm too old to do anything about it.

To remember thirteen is to remember a teenager crippled with teen neuroses. An internal monologue screaming 'You're fat, you're ugly, you're stupid, you're a freak.' Adolescent insanity that has little or no association with the facts. Unwilling, or unable to tell ourselves the truth, or the ignorant lack of self-awareness that prevents us from seeing ourselves clearly. Yet to look at twenty year old photographs is to see a handsome, slim, intelligent young man who could have done anything he wanted. Left to ask 'what if?' for the next twenty years or more.

It would be self-indulgent to look back on teen years at a succession of stunningly beautiful, charming and witty ex-girlfriends. Sadly, no such luxury can be afforded. Instead, only a litany of 'friendships' with the same cute, charismatic and sparkling young women. Too shy to press an advantage, too weak people skills to know when a girl really was interested. Left to ask 'what if?' for the next twenty years or more.

To be thirteen again! If only I had known then what I know now, I would have been unstoppable. A pubescent ball of terror, a danger to everyone including myself. With girlfriends aplenty, I would take from those who did not want to give and seize risks as though I was indestructible. Because as you get older, one of the things you learn is that you used to be incorruptible. And you aren't any more.

Darlington, 24th July 2009

Hung. Over.

By Mark McKnight

Not a good morning. My head is pounding like it's going to explode. I've thrown up more than I thought there was in there. Any kind of bright light feels like it is ripping my eyes in two. Anything louder than my own breath feels like a sledgehammer to my eardrums. I don't have the energy to even get out of bed and clean up the mess of bodily fluids I have made through the night. The euphoria of last night's liquor has been replaced by the dysphoria of this delirium tremens. And the flatulence!

Thirsty...need water...

Scientifically speaking, it might be too little blood sugar or dehydration or a bit of both. Whatever it is, I'm totally screwed up this morning.

Worse than all the weirdness that my body is going through this morning are the vagaries of last night's memories that are seeping back into my consciousness. It started badly – I happened to mention to my flatmates that I'd never had a hangover. Ever. So they had this great idea to get me so drunk that I couldn't avoid the DTs from which I'm now suffering. The idea was simple: to drink an entire week's alcohol in one night: 21 units in five hours. We'd start on fermented (beer, cider) and when we couldn't stomach any more of that, we'd move on to distilled (with a special emphasis in tequila for no other reason than they're selling it off cheap at the local off license).

My memory goes a bit hazy after the fifth pint. Unfortunately, I can piece things together from the text messages that I received last night during my bender. All of them, regrettably, from my ex-girlfriend.

"Errr...hi! Yeah, it's been a while. I'm gd. U?"
"Thanks. Not sure. Bit busy this week."
"Don't think that would be a good idea. Am with someone else now. Sorry."
"You don't need to be like that. We had some fun together but you need to move on."
"Please don't say that, even as a joke. Have you been drinking?"
"I'm not going to text back if you swear at me!"
"Apology accepted. But I still don't want to meet up. It would be a bad idea."
"Because you're drunk and can't deal with just friendship – you

always want more."

"Talk to me when you're sober, you jerk!"

"Screw you!"

"That's not what I meant and you know it. My boyfriend is here right now and he's been reading your messages. You better stop texting me!"

"You should be scared. He's the captain of the rugby team."

"How dare you! It's none of your f'ing business. We haven't been together for over a year now!"

"You bastard! Stop contacting me. I've had enough of your drunken text messages."

And then just one more from a number I didn't recognise:

"If you contact Alison again, I'll rip your head off, asshole!"

Hung. Over.

Darlington, 11th August 2009

Ears

By Mark McKnight

So I'm sitting at this low table, slouching back in these lilac leather recliners sofas. This joint is way too trendy for me. I usually feel out of place in this kind of a club but not tonight. Maybe because of the designer threads I'm wearing: blue jeans, black open neck shirt, brown cowboy boots. Anyway, we're celebrating. I don't fully understand why we're celebrating – I don't think it's my party but it's good to be here.

I think it must be some kind of retro seventies club. The disco ball, the faux fur and the conspicuously retro dance floor give it away. There doesn't seem to be any normal drinks here, and by normal I mean pints of Guinness. For that matter, there's no pints of lager, bitter, ale or cider either. This is not the type of club where they're likely to serve you a pint of the black stuff. More likely, they'll serve you cocktails, shots, wine... In other words, posh drinks. Once again, I don't feel out of place drinking my Long Island Iced Tea.

When I'm in a bar or a club, I love being the centre of attention. I like to crack my jokes, tell stories of past glories and generally keep the table enthralled by my craic. So that's what I do, keeping my companions entertained with a story about swimming with dolphins. It never happened, but as I always say, never let the truth get in the way of a good story.

Half way through my story, I realise that I'm not at this table 'alone'. As a matter of fact, there's this blonde girl sitting beside me. And she seems to think I'm a big deal. How do I know this? She keeps telling me and everyone at the table how cute my ears are. My ears? Really?

I've never really stopped to think too much about my ears. They've always been there and I've made a habit of cleaning them regularly, inside and out. No special attention to speak of, you understand. Yet all of a sudden, this hot, busty blonde lady thinks I'm great. Especially my ears. My ears? Really?

To be honest, she has rather nice ears herself. Although that's only one of her many stunning features. Those eyes, that hair, those lips, those boo...well, you get the idea.

And finally I get to the bit that I don't actually understand. Why is this girl sitting beside me telling everyone how cute my ears are? My ears? Really? There's clearly much better looking men sitting around the low table on the lilac leather sofas with the disco ball and the Long Island Iced Tea and all that. And then I realise the thing that hits me every time I have one of these encounters. Every time I'm sitting beside a beautiful woman. It's a dream.

Bollocks...

Or should I say, ears!

Still, it has made me look at my ears a little more closely in the bathroom mirror.

Darlington, 3rd November 2009

Belgium!

By Mark McKnight

Belgium!

I remember the first time I visited. Frankly, I was intoxicated. The smells, the sights, the sounds. In fact, there was a time when I was almost ready to abandon all and move to your fair shores and I think you might have welcomed me with open arms.

Childish, immature, broken, mischievous, I was all of the above. You? Not so much. I could feel it even back then – I was not ready to be a Belgian. Belgium was a place of stability. Neutrality. A place for grown ups. A place that would tolerate rather than embrace my impish humour and boyish ways.

Back then, I lacked a home. Somewhere to belong. Somewhere to be loved. I wonder if Belgium was offering that? Maybe I'll never know. There were people in Belgium who cared about me. Wanted to see the best for me. Held their tongue when I acted like a jerk because they loved me too much. And I wasn't ready to hear it anyway.

You don't count the cost of the sacrifices you make at the time. It is only in looking back that you see the reality of your decisions. That one was a costly one. I stood for a while looking at the border between my world and Belgium and made the decision not to cross. Made the decision to stay in my own world and to be my own person. The blessing and the curse of independence.

It took six long, harsh winters for me to pluck up the courage to re-apply for an entrance visa. Six winters wondering 'what if'? Six winters wondering what still might be. Twice, I had the application form filled in and still lacked the confidence to find out whether Belgium's borders still remained open. I always knew Belgium was there, built up to a virtual Elysian Fields of the mind. It was all that was wrong with this life and all that would be right about the next.

After those six long winters, I changed. I found that I had the confidence I needed to resubmit. But wouldn't you know, their immigration policies had changed. No longer an open border. With strict guidelines on who gets in and who doesn't, I no longer qualify. My past record counted against me. All the things I did from years ago were dragged up as I watched. It seemed like fun to begin with, remembering all the daft stunts from another era. But as it continued, a picture was painted of a person that I no longer am. A picture of a person who Belgium were not interested in having as a citizen. A painful reminder that I had my chance and I blew it.

And now the home that I thought I had found seems like a prison cell. As I decorate, it feels like I'm entrenching myself. Digging in to a position that I never sought and no longer want. Because it's not Belgium, and never will be.

Belgium!

Cresswell, 19th February 2010

Found A Frog

By Mark McKnight

Mam, mam, guess what happened today?

I found a frog...

Well, because me and Timmy were on our way home and took a short-cut across the fields. Timmy got his boot stuck in some mud and we had to leave it there 'cos we couldn't get it out and he had to walk home with only one welly on. His sock was black when he got home and it was meant to be white...

No, mam I'm not finished. There's something even more exciting. We got into a field and there were no cows or sheep – just a couple of giraffes eating the very top leaves off of a tree. Then one of them turned around and asked Timmy what happened to his boot...

Why don't you believe me, mam? Anyway, there's something even better than that. There were these weird giant circles drawn in the grass and guess what drew them? That's right – a spaceship. How did you know? We even saw the spaceship leaving but when we waved at the aliens they came back and spoke to us and told us to make sure we brush our teeth twice every day...

I dunno. That's just what they told us...

Timmy asked them if we could go to space with them but they said no 'cos it was nearly dark and our mams would be wondering where we were...

No, it was still daylight when they left us...

It's dark now because we couldn't come straight home...

We had to go to the police station...

'Cos when we were going passed the jeweller's in the high street, we saw two men robbing the shop...

Well, Timmy took his other boot off and threw it at them. I think they got a bit scared because they ran off when they heard the sirens coming...

They said they tried to phone you but that a bolt of lightning had hit the police station and all the phones had stopped working...

Well they brought me home in their police car and it was parked just outside the door about an hour ago. I was about to get out when a call came over the radio that an earthquake had just hit the school and the police forgot that I was in the back and drove to the school which is knocked down completely...

I know, I won't be able to go to school any more because

it's not even there now...

They said that it wasn't going to be on the news because it was probably secret agents that caused the earthquake and since they're secret, they don't want anyone finding out...

And then when I got back home I had to fight some pirates just to get into our house. I think there must have been about a hundred of them.

Anyway, mum, do you have an old shoebox I can borrow?

Because I need somewhere to put Eric.

Haven't you been listening? Eric is my frog that I found.

Cresswell, 19th February 2010

Magneto

By Mark McKnight

"How are you? I'm looking for a magneto for a Lister D engine."

That's how it starts, or something along those lines. I grew up working on vintage engines with my dad. And we spent countless Autumn Saturday mornings at auto jumbles on God-forsaken car parks surrounded by the slow decay of a heavy industrial past looking for the one thing that's probably not there in the first place. A wiring loom for a 1953 Ford Popular. Or a sump nut for a 1948 Nuffield M4 tractor. Or a fuel gauge for a Triumph T120 motorbike.

In reality, what you're looking for is never there. But auto jumbles aren't about parts. Auto jumbles are about people. Men who have had grease under their fingernails for the last 70 years. So when you ask for whatever it is you're looking for, they won't have one, but they know a fella who knows another fella who was once married to a woman who's father worked for the company who manufactured the part that you're looking for.

He writes your number on the back of an bus ticket that's in his pocket with a pen that lays down ink about 30% of the time. He promises that he'll get back to you this evening after he's had his dinner.

So you wait...and wait...and wait. A month has gone by, you've been to three more auto jumbles and your number has been written three more times on a piece of card torn from an air filter box, a burger wrapper and a flyer advertising a psychic evening at a pub you'll never go to in a village you've never heard of.

Then out of the blue one evening, as you're tucking into a bowl of stew you get a call to say that he's found just the man who can help you. You pull up at a darkened farmhouse to be greeted by three baying hounds. Before long, a young buck answers the door and tells you it's his father you'll be looking for. But he says, "Go on round back to the shed – he'll be there in a minute." You wait outside the shed for 25 minutes until an auld fella who's just about beat wanders across the yard.

Small talk aside, you enter the shed which turns out to be an Aladdin's cave of auto jumble, most of which hasn't moved in the last 20 years. A few minutes digging reaches a steel cabinet at the back of the shed with shelves sagging from the weight. There, in the back corner is the very part you've spent six months looking for.

"Sure it'll only sit there for the next 30 years as well. You may as well just take it." In jubilation, you spend three days trying to fit the part and make it work only to discover that it's a clockwise turn magneto you need, rather than this one which is an anti-clockwise turn.

Back to square one!

Darlington, 9th April 2010

Stud Of The Year

By Mark McKnight

I'm really not a big fan of nightclubs. I'd rather find a pub with some live music and enjoy a good night's craic. I've even been known to get on the stage and play a song or two meself. But that's not always how it works out. For most girls like to dance, don't they?

Back in the old days, there used to be two nightclubs across the road from each other – the Eg and the Bot. We liked the Eg – there was usually less fights, although the night I'm thinking of, it took me about 10 mins to actually get in. Not because there was a queue, but the bouncers were beating seven bells out of a fella who thought he was hard. And he kept getting up and fighting back. I was hoping he'd just stay down I could get in the freaking nightclub!

Eventually, I got in and had my ass felt on the way to the bar. This was also the night that I heard 'It's Raining Men' for the first dance. There I was boogeying away until it hit the chorus. Sure they were all laughing at me as I made a quick exit from the dance floor.

Anyway, there's always a few perves around and one had taken a shine to my friend Helen. We did the sneaky dance move where I put myself between him and her and he gets the message which is just as well for I wasn't for fighting. Now you have to know that Helen is blonde and it's a lucky man who ends up with her. Next thing Helen and I are chatting at the side of the dance floor, having a drink and generally enjoying the evening.

We call it a night not too late for I have to be up early the morrow morning. No night cap or any of that carry on – tomorrow night is going to be a big one and I can't risk a hangover.

So next day, we're sitting with some other friends having lunch and one of them says, "Who was that good looking blonde cuddy we seen you with last night Mark?" And I says, "That's just Helen – she's just a friend." And I thought that was that.

So then that night, is the annual music department formal dinner and they're giving out all their daft awards. And of course I'm making jokes and generally slabberin' for I never win anything like that – popular enough but not that popular. And they announce the award for Stud Of The Year. "This person is a dark horse – he never really talks about one particular girl and he has lots who are his 'friend' but we think it's more than that – all these girls who are just his friends! Stud Of The Year goes to Mark McKnight!"

I still have it and all – it's on my shelf there beside King Solomon the monkey.

Darlington, 9th April 2010

Internet Dating

By Mark McKnight

Everybody's looking for the same thing – companionship, love, someone to care for them. And in this day and age, it ain't easy to meet someone. You go to bars, or hang out in the supermarket, go to places where you think you might meet a lady but it just doesn't click. They just aren't there, or you don't have the guts to talk to them, or even worse it's turned into a cruising spot for older gay gentlemen and you unwittingly end up getting a whole lot more than you bargained for.

So you think, 'What about the Internet?' And you justify it to yourself – in this day and age, websites are as valid a place to meet someone as anywhere else. You can meet weirdoes at a bar as easily as you can online. You get online, you google for a while and find a site that you like the look of. Sign up for the 30 day free trial. Spend most of an evening creating an eye catching profile that's going to woo the ladies.

Next night, you spend hours and hours browsing through profiles. You start with the ones that are close by – within twenty or thirty miles. There's one or two that you like the look of but then you widen your search pattern. A hundred miles. Anywhere in the country. Then anywhere on the continent. Then anywhere in the world.

There's a few profiles that stand out and catch your eye, so you try to send them a carefully worded message. Except that's where they sting you. You can only contact people if you have a paid membership. So you splash out the princely sum of £24.99 for six months' membership and before long you're sending messages telling women how much you enjoyed reading their profile. And you even get one or two responses back. Nothing that really interests you though. Nice enough, but sixes or sevens rather than nines or tens. So you go back to the surfing, trying to find at least some eights.

You lose interest after a few weeks and more or less give up – you're not making any progress so why bother. Anyway, you've got other things you need to spend your time doing. Of course, the site emails you every time someone else tries to make contact which is irregular to say the least.

But one day, you get an email from the site to say that they've found a one hundred percent match for you. This woman is a couple of year younger than you and even lives in the same post code area. You share some interests, and their compatibility matching has decided you will make an excellent pair. Without wasting any time, you sign in to the site and it doesn't take long before you find this mystery lady's profile. There's only one problem – you see the picture and you realise why the post code is the same – it's your sister!

Darlington, 17th April 2010

The Brush Off

By Mark McKnight

So a couple of months ago, I had this 'epiphany moment' when I realised that I was well known in the area as something of a workaholic. I mean, don't get me wrong, I love my job. But that's not what I want to be known as. I'd rather be known as someone who has time for people and who cares about my friends.

Anyway, the very next day I press the snooze button one too many times and end up getting out of the shower at 10:26am. The problem is, it's Harvest Festival at church. Four minutes is clearly not enough time to get dressed, put some product on my hair, find some tins to put on the table for the Harvest collection and get to church. And I don't want all those old ladies tutting at me for being unkempt, empty handed and most of all late. Tut. Tut. Tut.

I decide to go to the only church in town that I know starts at 11:00am. I'm just in the door when I'm welcomed by a very pretty blonde girl. Oh, and the rest of their young adults too. Boy, do they like to welcome people. So much for slipping in the back without being noticed! I almost straight away have this little new group of friends. Which is just great and we all hang out, go to some parties, see a couple of movies and finish a pub quiz with an embarrassingly low score together. They become known as AFNF (Aforementioned Fantastic New Friends) on Facebook.

And then the pretty blonde girl starts communicating. Just the odd 'Like' on Facebook, and then Facebook chat and the it escalates to text messages. What I'd call real actual communication. She's young but after consultation with my dad (who married a much younger woman) I'm not that bothered. And for a solid couple of weeks we text. Regularly. We even go out twice on what could nearly be called 'dates'. On the first, for coffee, she is clearly flirting. And so am I, so that's OK. On the second, to a concert, we're in public so it's not quite the same, especially with so many people she knows around. But I drive her home and she's completely into me. Body language, the way she's communicating, all that.

But you and I know that all good things must come to an end, and in my love life that is often sooner rather than later. The phone goes dead. No texts, no calls, no Facebook, no emails. Silence. My jolly invitations for coffee go unanswered. My jokes with no 'Lol' to reply. And then, after two days, it arrives. The brush off!

What happened? We may never know. My guess? She freaking out because she's just figured out that a boy likes her. Maybe someone told her. Maybe she figured it out for herself. And then at the end of her brush off text she puts a kiss. They're a funny bunch, girls.

Darlington, 12th November 2010

Your Smile Lights Up My Life

By Mark McKnight

Your smile lights up my life. It's been that way ever since the day we met. I've known this for many years now and few can understand how it makes me feel when you walk past, whisper you love me and flash me your million dollar smile.

Truth be told, there's about another dozen people who make me smile the way you do, but you're the only one who smiles back the way you do. I remember times (and I can still see them in your eyes) when I never saw that smile. Days when you were tortured by melancholy. Hurt by friends. Short on cash and short on friends. And we journeyed through those days together. And I would have done anything to make you smile again.

I still would.

Your smile lights up my life. And I know why. Because I see in you, all that I have invested. Hundreds of pounds of my own money to pay for your education. Enough hours spent with you. Not yet enough hours praying for you and worrying about you. Plenty of sweat, about a pint of blood and just one small tear. The tear that comes from the realisation that I've invested so much of me in you that there may not be enough of me left for me.

You have endured hardships in your life that the likes of me will never know. The harsh daily grind of poverty. The relentless Africa sun. But we can work together. We can lift you up to be something more than you could have been alone. I have the investment of my time, my money, myself. You have the intense, unbridled, mind-blowing, desperate, powerful potential of youth. Together, you will be more. You will achieve more. You are more.

And me? Surely you being more means me being less? Or together can we both be more. I wonder if this is more of an even trade than I ever thought possible? There's a joy that you bring. Just being in the same city as you, knowing that you smile when you think about me is enough. Knowing that I've made a difference. To you. Not an organisation or a programme or a fund. Your life is changed for the better because of me. And not just my money but all the other stuff too – the time and the blood and the sweat and the tears. Just that knowledge is all that I need in return.

That's what it comes down to. That's why your smile lights up my life. Because behind it, I know what that smile means. That you <u>know</u> what you mean to me. That when you say you love me, you know the cost at which it has come. And though there's still plenty of hopes and hurts and life and laughter, your smile makes it all worthwhile. That's all I ask for in return.

Your smile lights up my life. And I hope mine lights your life too.

Lugala, 1st January 2011

Happily Unhappily Single

By Mark McKnight

There's this family we know with four daughters called the Katigos. We used to visit them more or less every Sunday afternoon without fail. Actually, it was more because they always had a pretty good Sunday lunch on the go that was available for all visitors. Oh, and looking back, my friends were trying to fix me up but as with the rest of my friends, they have failed completely!

One of my favourite memories on a Sunday afternoon was going for Rolex with Susan. Or the ka-boy that used to come around selling his roasted maize. I guess he must have raised enough capital to move on to something bigger and better, because he doesn't come around any more. We usually cleaned him out of about half his stock what with the whole family plus various hangers on (including myself).

Liz told me she was taking me out for Valentine's Day once. Truthfully, I was too scared to refuse and that has been a source of much merriment for the last eight years. We went for ice cream at a nice hotel in town. When we came back, they were sweeping the yard with giant burning branches. Apparently, it's the best way to get rid of fire ants. Trust me – you don't want those things crawling on you! The year after, James screwed all our Valentine's plans up by getting married that day.

Last Sunday, we went around there again. I haven't laughed as hard in a long, long time. Catching up with old friends, hearing stories from the past few years. And occasionally a sharing of the trials and humour of living through war. Like how Liz has two birthdays because her mum and dad can't agree – her birth certificate was lost when they had to flee the soldiers.

Yet even after eight years, none of the Katigo sisters has found a husband. To be fair, only three of them are of marriageable age – Susan is only seventeen now but Liz, Jane and Joyce are all still looking for the man of their dreams. Yet from a very traditional culture, they will not be the ones to initiate a relationship – they must be courted and won, and there's a whole lot of other baggage that I'll never understand.

It's interesting when happily but unhappily single people get together. The talk often turns to whom they are looking for and how they will know when they've found them. And this is helpful. Mutual support. Empathy. But there are also often glib answers from those who have found a spouse already that are at best unhelpful and at worst downright insulting. And they can laugh together, encourage one another and have a good time in the process. But that doesn't keep you warm at night. It forgets the gnawing loneliness of an empty house and an empty bed.

And the Katigo sisters, like myself remain happily unhappily single. May 2011 be the year of husbands and wives!

Lugala, 6th January 2011

Money

By Mark McKnight

It's a funny old thing, is money. The less you have, the more you learn about it's value and how much it's really worth.

Once upon a time, I was dirt poor. Not dirt poor like the little kids who run around shouting 'Mzungu, Mzungu' but poor enough. We used to buy a 25¢ bottle of soda between two of us because we couldn't afford to buy one each. We took rich missions teams to expensive restaurants and prayed that they would buy us lunch. On the whole, this policy paid off. Once or twice it didn't and we had to buy our own meal! We had to bargain hard with the street traders because although they assumed we were rich because we were white, the truth was that we could just about to afford what they were selling and needed to buy at African prices just to survive.

There were 15 people living in my house at one time and it was only by God's grace that we all survived. I used to buy a 50kg sack of rice and another of beans and they'd be gone in 2 weeks. We quickly learned that there were different grades of rice and the cheapest was full of rocks and grit. The second from cheapest was therefore the appropriate one to buy.

But it taught what was important to us. We learned that proper Heinz ketchup was something we were willing to invest in. That bottled mineral water was not. Especially after the discovery of water for 100/= (aka vanilla water) and water for 50/= (now discredited as a false economy!). We learned there are some people who can be trusted and there are many more who cannot. There are some that will lie about the death of their own child in order to rip you off.

These are things I learned five years ago. Nowadays, I'm neither rich nor poor. My bank accounts are neither awash with unspent cash nor biting at the heels of overdraft limits. For the first time in my life (except for my student days, and that was only thanks to student loans – another false economy), I have disposable income.

What I learned back then was that I am no island. Others have invested their time and money in me and now I bear that same responsibility. I've made a few anonymous donations. I've invested in an African poultry business more because I have the money to do so rather than because I think I'll make any significant profits. I'm putting a kid through university here.

But in comparison, I spend a whole lot on myself. There's

a bass guitar that I have my eye on that would keep Dorah at uni for well over a year. My car cost more than her entire course will. The human condition is a constant struggle between altruism and selfishness. And at the end of the day, it's mostly selfishness that wins.

It's a funny old thing, is money!

Lugala, 6th January 2011

Blind Date From Hell

By Mark McKnight

"We have to get Marko a girl."

So says the popular wisdom of my so-called friends. As if finding a young lady would be the answer to all of my problems. Maybe it would, or maybe it wouldn't. I suppose it probably comes from an semi-altruistic position. They care about me and want to see me happy.

Anyway, loathe as I usually am to get involved in fix-ups, in a moment of weakness, I succumbed to the pressure and agreed to go on a blind date. This time, the pressure wasn't just from a single friend. This time, six separate people decided that this was the girl for me. In retrospect, these friends either didn't know me or more likely, as the events that unfolded are about to show, had never met this delightful lady.

The warning signs were there, to be sure. Like the fact that her choice for our date was to visit the West Cumbrian Pencil Museum. Now I'm not against pencils. Or even museums. But on a first date? To be fair, the gift shop and café were second to none. And as Pencil Museums go, it was probably in the top ten. But I echo, on a first date? And she was really interested in the pencils. Freakishly interested. Telling me all about graphite and Borrowdale and Conte and quadrachromics.

By the end of the tour, my mind was beginning to wander and my mouth was beginning to yawn, but I managed to hold it together over coffee in the coffee shop attached to the museum. It was then that she began telling me about the animals. I'm not much of an animal lover but this was just ridiculous. After a while, I counted at least eight different pets that she was constantly talking about as if they were actual people. As far as I could make out, there were three dogs, two cats, a hamster, a budgie and a Chile Flame Tarantula. The tarantula (for some reason named Peter) seemed to be the favourite. In fact, there were also some hints that he might even be in her handbag.

After a couple of hours I'd had enough. On a fairly thin pretext, I make my excuses and try to leave, but she won't let me go until she's got my number. In a panic, I give her my real number and that was the biggest mistake I ever made. Before I even make it home, the first texts come through...

Had a wonderful time tonight. Hope to see you again soon.
You there? Please text back. Had a great time!
Why aren't you texting? Was fun.

What's wrong with you? Text back!
You jerk! We could have been something.
What an asshole. I wasted a whole day with you.
And from there it goes from bad to worse. More swear words,
more threats, more ugly text messages. I still get one from here
every now and then reminding me of my blind date from hell.

Darlington, 8th-9th January 2011

Break In

By Mark McKnight

I came in the door just after lunch yesterday and there's this guy standing in my hallway. He didn't skip a beat and straight away he told me that he'd seen three lads trying to break in the back door of my house. He'd scared them away and that's why he was in the house. He took me out through my office and showed me where they had broken the door. He even shook my hand and told me his name. The police were already on their way. Then he said, 'I'll just get my lass out of the car if that's OK.'

He was very plausible. I believed every single word he said, fully expecting him to come back in with his girlfriend. But then a minute passed. And then another. Shit! Shit, shit, shit! That was him. He looked me in the eye while lying. It all happened so fast, which I suppose is the way it was meant to go down. He was gone before I fully understood what was happening. He even gave himself a couple of minutes head start by telling me he'd already phoned the police.

The police were great – they didn't judge us for having gone out without switching the alarm on. They didn't even tell me I was an idiot for believing this guy (which I was). Of course, there was a parade of coppers through our living room over the course of the day – C.I.D., C.S.I. and a couple of uniformed bobbies. (C.S.I. Darlo doesn't quite have the same ring to it).

In the living room, he'd packed up all of our laptops ready to take with him. A couple of cameras, some cash that had been lying around and some jewellery too. Someone up there must have been looking after me. If I hadn't walked in when I did, he probably would have had the lot.

Truthfully, I'm not that bothered about the physical stuff. I'm insured. Cameras can be replaced. Laptops bought anew. What would have hurt the most would be the loss of data. Photos. Videos. Irreplaceable memories.

Worse still is what he's done to the sanctity of my home. Every moment I'm thinking about whether the windows are locked and if the alarm is working properly. I check the front door every time I pass it to make sure it's not open. I've thought seriously about buying a safe. Not that I have anything valuable enough to put in a safe, but it makes you paranoid. Passports. Credit cards. Keys. I've put keys in safe places that I don't even know what they open!

I'm a fairly level guy but when you're in the house alone, it makes you think. Like what if he'd been armed? What if I caught him with the laptops in his hands? What if he was drunk or stoned? I don't care what atheist reads this, my God was looking after me yesterday. Things could have finished up so much worse.

Darlington, 15th January 2011

Do You Know What It Means?

By Mark McKnight

Do you know what it means to miss New Orleans? I do!

It's almost twelve years since I went there. Supposedly I was studying business, but the reality was that I spent more time playing jazz and gospel music than I did actually studying. Somehow, I still managed to leave with straight A's.

Dillard University is an HBCU – a Historically Black College/University. Let me tell you, that was an interesting cultural experience for a someone like me from Northern Ireland who had hardly seen a black person before except on TV. Back then, I didn't have a single black friend.

So on the thin pretext of studying business and with saxophone in hand, I set off to the deep south. It was the first time I'd been away from home by myself. And what a year it was. I played jazz with buskers on the streets of the French Quarter outside St. Louis Cathedral. I ate beignets from Café du Monde in the middle of the night during Mardi Gras because I missed the last bus home. I walked up and down Bourbon Street as girls bared their breasts for beads and wondered what kind of a place this was, where every building was a bar or a strip club or a sex shop. I went out on the bayous and swamps and visited old-time southern plantations. I made a whole heap of black friends, missed the boat on a couple of romances, tried my first daiquiri and grew up more than I ever would have if I'd just finished my degree and ambled into obscurity.

A wise man once said that when you travel, you never come all the way home again. And he was right. You see, New Orleans was my first taste of the world. Of all the exciting, mystifying, exhilarating, frightening, confusing, incredibly things that are out there. Away from where I grew up. Apart from what I know. Beyond what I understand.

And so I spent the next ten years drifting around the world. Always with some thin pretext of why I was there but in reality just enjoying the experience. There were always new people to meet and new adventures to have. I found some of my best friends in North America. Africa stole my heart. And then England dragged me back, kicking and screaming.

I don't regret any of it. Every journey, every mistake, every friendship has led me here. And I hope will lead me further. But sometimes, I yearn for those days when everything was fresh and new. My whole life was ahead of me. Those hot, humid days of a Louisiana summer when life was filled with untold potential.

One day I'll go back to New Orleans. I'll pay ten dollars to request 'The Saints' at Preservation Hall, catch some beads, eat some fried oysters on Bourbon Street, avoid the strip clubs and fix forever in my mind those reasons why I know what it means to miss New Orleans.

Darlington, 18th January 2011

Burns Night

By Mark McKnight

My old grandfather, God rest his soul, was born and raised a Scot. Just before he died, he made it back to Edinburgh for Hogmany. The airline wouldn't let him fly because he was in such poor health so Margot strapped him in the front seat of the Nissan Primera, put the wheelchair in the boot and off they set by boat to Caledonia. We went round for dinner the day after he came back and he was buzzing, he'd had such a good time. The trip itself damn near killed him, and he went downhill pretty quickly after that. But he was made up that he'd gotten back to Scotland once more before he died.

So this year, in honour of Granddad Fergusson, I hosted a Burns Night Supper. 'The Horse' invites along these two girls that he knows. I'm trying to get some music going (and can I say, nobody was impressed by my choice of the Regimental Band of the Royal Scots Dragoon Guards). I haven't showered. I stink a bit. And the doorbell rings.

We had a solid evening – everyone was suitably impressed with my haggis, neeps and tatties. Jon made a load of shortbread and we inaugurated our two tier cake stand. Oh, and this girl laughed at my jokes. A lot! Not enough that I'd think she's mental or anything, but enough to make me notice her. And when I say notice her, I mean I sent her a little note a couple of days later:

"Dear Emma, you seem like a really cool person and I'd love to get to know you better. If you want to grab a coffee some time, my number is 07866123456. Mark."

That's not my real number, obviously. I'm not going to print that in a book! Not exactly a love note and not really a piece of literature either, but enough to serve my purpose. And apparently she was smiling when she read it. Which is good!

About six hours later, the text comes in. "Hi Mark, it's just Emma. Thanks v much for the letter, v kind. Yeah sure coffee would be good. :-)" The punctuation and grammar isn't great, but we'll let that slide. And after a few more texts, I have a date. Next Saturday afternoon. I have a few tricks up my sleeve – depends on how long she wants to spend with me.

And I'm doing my best to not build it up to more than it is. But I had this weird dream last night about her. And we polished off a couple of bottles of wine last night and I got plenty of advice, of mixed quality. Shave. Don't play with your ears. Don't tell her about my dressing up box. Be myself. Don't be myself!

It's been some time since I've been on an actual date. This feels like a new departure. But 501 words are gone – I'm sure there will be another story, whether good or bad!

Darlington, 1st February 2011

Awkward

By Mark McKnight

I saw this girl in church one day. A blonde who was singing in the band. And she was gorgeous and with the distinct lack of decent Christian women (certainly around here), I was waiting for someone to introduce me to her. But nobody did. Once, I was at a concert and she was sitting right behind me. My friend was sitting beside her and I know she knows her. But still no introduction. Facebook kept telling me that I knew her so one day in early December I decided to take matters into my own hands:

We haven't been properly introduced, but Facebook keeps telling me that I know you!
I've been along to your church a few times and I've been hanging out with some of the guys who I think you know.
I'd love to go for coffee with you some time and get to know you if you're interested.
Mark.

And within 20 minutes, I had a reply:
Hi mark, sorry about the brief reply but I'm at work at the mo, yea that would be cool some time, just let me know whens good and we can see if we can sort something :)

But I didn't think it all through properly – the two weeks before Christmas are the silly season in church. So we weren't able to get anything organised before the the New Year. I hadn't heard from her in a while and had more or less given up hope. But then, almost three weeks later:
Hi Mark, hope you have had a great chrsitmas and new year :-) so sorry i havent been in touch, things have been craaazzyy!!!! Still up for that coffee if you are... would wednesday morn be any good for you?? :-)

Except I was in Africa at the time:
Doh! I'm in Uganda until Friday! And I saw your message about an hour ago and was thinking, 'It's Tuesday. I'll upload these photos after breakfast and then reply.' I've just realised it's already Wednesday! So no can do for today, I'm afraid.

But yes, I'm still up for it. Next week some time? :)

Nothing!

Just looking at my diary for the coming week. I'm free any morning this week. :-)

Nothing!

This week?
I have a fairly flexible few days. After 3 on Wednesday is no good and Thursday lunchtime is a major no-no. My bosses are all away on retreat so I can reorganise anything else!
Mark :-)

Nothing!

And then, I meet another girl. I plan a date. I'm out buying a new pair of boots to make sure I'm looking sharp. I see the ones I like, look up for a sales assistant and there she is. Talk about awkward! It takes me completely by surprise that I've bought the boots from her and left the shop without ever actually acknowledging the fact that we have unfinished business.
And I laugh almost all the way home at the ridiculousness of the whole thing.

Darlington, 1st February 2011

Chosen

By Mark McKnight

In my culture, life isn't easy for women. There's always another job to do – fetch the water, prepare the tea, sweep the compound, wash the clothes... A girl is luck if she lives with their parents. The unlucky ones live with a step-father. The wretched live with an auntie or an uncle or some other person who will take them in. The lucky wretch will only be pierced by sharp words. The unlucky wretch endures a leather belt or the back of a hand. The wretched wretch must endure much more. Unspeakable things.

But once in her lifetime, there is the most wonderful chance for a girl to escape her miserable life. In the dry season after she has turned eighteen, every maiden in the kingdom must participate in the reed dance.

The celebration lasts for three days. On the first day, we all report to the queen mother's palace. After we've been stripped naked, a team of heavy handed soldiers check to see who is lying about their virginity. There are all kinds of stories about girls who have been dragged off and raped by the soldiers before being thrown in a truck and dumped back in their village. The queen mother watches while the fat soldiers grope and finger all the prettiest girls. A couple of girls are dragged away wailing and screaming.

For those that escape the ugly pervert soldiers, next day we are sent with our knives (that symbolise our virginity) to cut some reeds. The reeds are four yards long and each girl returns with a bundle of reeds on her head. We keep one of the reeds for the reed dance but spend the rest of the day repairing the royal compound with the reeds we have collected.

We work late into the night but rather than retire to sleep, we spend the rest of the night helping each other to look our best. After plaiting each other's hair, we rub our skins with paint made from oil and ochre. By morning we should all be ready to perform the reed dance for the king. Around our ankles, we wear anklets made of a special seed that rattles. Around our waist, we wear a short beaded skirt that our mothers or aunties have helped us make. Many of us wear necklaces and other jewellery made from shells.

As the sun peeks over the horizon, we perform the reed dance for the king. The dance is energetic – every one of us wants to attract the king's eye. Although it's a bitterly cold morning, soon our bare breasts glisten with drops of sweat. We dance for at least an hour before the king rises from his throne. He dips his fingers in an bowl of ash mixed with water. We turn to face away from him – he will daub one girl's back with the ash, signifying that she will be his next wife.

We wait for what seems like forever. And then he chooses....me!

Darlington, 3rd February 2011

Waiting

By Mark McKnight

The time ticks slowly by. This last week has seemed like a year. Waiting. A roller coaster of emotions, not only because of you. But the clocks have slowly spun their way around eleven times. This morning, it is a slow motion version of life that I experience.

I've started tidying the house. Twice. But my heart isn't in it. I shift a few things from room to room, potter a bit and then decide to do something else. I have spent thirteen of the last fifteen minutes staring into space. Thinking. Daydreaming.

Why has today drawn me out such? This afternoon, I will have coffee with you. A date. My first for a while if you don't count the couple of false starts. Am I nervous? Not so much. Okay, then. A bit! Well what about excited? Of course I'm excited. A lot. But that's not the main thing I'm feeling. Apprehensive? Punching above my weight? That's not it either.

Impatient. That's the word. I am feeling impatient. Along with all those other things. I'm ahead of the curve for this daate – I scouted the venue on Tuesday, had to work on Wednesday, washed my shirt on Thursday and ironed it on Friday. The motor is clean inside and out. I've drawn out some cash which is in my wallet ready.

Sure, I need to shower and shave but it's still a bit early for that. I could do some work. As if my mind could concentrate on anything except for this afternoon. I could try tidying once more – last night's dinner party has left it's mark and there's still work to do. But I just can't be bothered.

Minutes seem like hours. Hours seem like days.

I can handle the waiting – I'm used to waiting. The thing I don't want to accept is that when two o'clock comes around, suddenly time will speed up again. Faster than it's ever been. Hours will seem like minutes and minutes will seem like nanoseconds. Before I know it, we'll be saying goodbye and who knows what then. Another date? A kiss on the hand? Valentine's Day?

I (and her too) have spent much of the last week weighed down by both the pressure and the potential. The words 'DON'T SCREW THIS UP!' screaming in our minds. And the excitement of 'THIS COULD BE IT!' whispering on the edge of our hearts. Like an angel and devil whispering into each ear. And truth be told, the longer I have to wait, the longer I have to listen to the little red devil and twist my mind in knots.

So I wait. For there is nothing else I can do. Writing this helps pass the time.

But it looks like the time for waiting has passed. The time for showering and shaving is at hand. And then the time for driving and the time for parking. And then the time of dating and worst of all lastly the time for parting.

Darlington, 3rd February 2011

Royal Wedding

By Mark McKnight

It's difficult to put your finger on quite what it is, but princely matrimony seems to capture a nation's imagination. And when it's the second in line to the throne, it's going to be a big one. Those of us old enough will remember the fairytale that was the union of this prince's two parents. These events only come along once in a lifetime. We haven't had a state occasion like this since his mother's funeral. And that brought all the mentalists out of the woodwork – the newspapers lapped them up.

But nothing brings out the crazies quite like a royal wedding. And every single one of them has an idea for a party. Now don't get me wrong, I don't begrudge the royalists. The money the royal family brings into this country from tourism alone makes them value for money. But there's two types of enthusiasts of the sovereignty. The first own commemorative plates from the coronation and coins from the last royal wedding. They have coffee table books about the Queen Mother. They like to buy royal tat off the online auction sites. They are mostly harmless.

There's another type, though. The type that you don't find out about until it's almost too late. Without realising it, I took one on a date this afternoon. Things were going well until she told me her plans for the royal wedding. And at that point bright red alarm bells started ringing.

"I can't wait for the royal wedding," she said. "It will be great to get a long weekend off work, what with the extra bank holiday."

"Really," I said. "Have you got plans for the weekend?"

"Oh yes. Some people aren't that bothered about the royal wedding but I can't wait. All my girl friends are going to come around to my house. We're going to have canapés and champagne cocktails. It's going to be wonderful. The girl who's going to be the princess is beautiful and we can't wait to see her dress."

"So you'll all be analysing her hair and dress and jewellery and stuff then?"

"Yes. In fact, we're all going to buy old wedding dresses from charity shops and put them on while we're watching it on the telly. It's going to be fabulous!"

Strangely enough, the date we were on started to go downhill quite quickly after she told me that little nugget. We strayed away from the subject of the royal family but that image was so frighteningly imprinted on my mind, that when it came time to say goodbye, we did just that. Said goodbye. Most likely there will <u>not</u> be a second date to look forward to. And I even ironed my favourite shirt!

My own plans for the royal wedding? I'm not sure yet, but you can be sure that it will not involve renting a tuxedo, wearing a cummerbund, eating canapés, drinking champagne cocktails or watching the royal wedding on the telly! Although, I may buy myself a dress!

Darlington, 5th February 2011

Ridiculous Vegetable Chopping Injury

By Mark McKnight

I did something very stupid the other day. What has become affectionately known and the ridiculous vegetable chopping injury. We had some guests coming over for dinner, so I thought I'd make a nice sausage casserole. I have this thing called a mandoline, which does a fine job of chopping veg. In fact it can dice an onion in no time flat. Which is exactly what I was doing when my fingers got a bit too close to the blade.

It turns out those vegetable slicers are just as good at slicing fingers as they are onions. Of course, I'm in the house by myself and there was blood everywhere. It was touch and go whether or not I was going to Accident & Emergency. But I'm a first aider, and I figured that since it was sliced cleanly, there wasn't much they could do for me that I couldn't do for myself. So I whacked a bandage on it and hoped for the best.

Of course, the casserole was ruined. I mean, I fished the piece of finger out, but nobody wants to eat a meal that has that kind of history. I had to throw the entire batch in the bin!

The thing is, you don't realise how valuable your fingers are until you can't use them. I can't tie my shoelaces very well, I have to put a plastic bag over it in the shower and even shaving is a struggle. Using a knife and fork is impossible and signing my name is a new adventure every day, never mind trying to write anything of length.

What I find the most difficult is the fact that I'm not going to be able to play the guitar again for ages. There have been some suggestions that I take up the drums, which is about as good as it's going to get for a while. My fingertip is so tender, I'm not even going to try to press down a guitar string for a while. And who knows what it will be like when I do.

The crazy thing is that when I was a teenager, I went to one single martial arts lesson. I can't remember what it was – Ju Jitsu or Tae Kwondo or something. And I remember thinking, 'As a musician, this would be a really fabulous way to break a finger and destroy a perfectly good music career.' And now, just when things were starting to move for me, I'm crippled by a ridiculous vegetable chopping injury.

I've noticed myself a lot more nervous around knives – cutting cheese or bread is difficult with a bandaged finger, but the blade itself is a worry to me.

It's not even a bad injury. I lost a bit of blood and it will be tender for a while. It's not really worth sympathy (and few people have given it). Perhaps this is a sign from above that I need to retire! Or at least try something different.

Darlington, 11th March 2011

Plus One

By Mark McKnight

Family weddings. They're a law unto themselves. There's two schools of thought. Firstly, and eminently more popular, is to get completely tanked. Best case scenario: you won't remember much of what happens. Worst case scenario, you embarrass yourself in front of your family and never live it down. I have a sister who is still struggling with that one from a wedding eleven years ago.

The problem is that there's some of the family who are just lovely – a joy to be around, with wit, grace and poise. Then there's the rest of the family who we just can't imagine how we're related to. The cousin-in-law who is abrasive and not interested in anyone's opinion but her own. The auntie who puts on airs and only talks to me because she has to. They are the reason most of the family turn to the demon drink.

For our most recent family wedding, I decided to try for a different solution. In retrospect, even the worst case scenario of the alcohol solution would have been preferable to what I came up with. About four months ago, I got the invitation to my cousin's wedding. Of course, it's always wonderful to share with somebody in their nuptials. But it's the plus one that always messes me up. When you've been single as long as I have, Mark +1 sucks.

And so I came up with the second school of thought in how to deal with a family wedding. Of course, everyone has something that their family is on their back about – too much wanderlust, carrying too much weight or not producing any grandkids. For me, it's the continued lack of a girlfriend. Like that's my fault! I had a foolproof idea that was going to get the family off my back permanently. I'd start a rumour. Of course, with families it doesn't need a whole lot to get them gossiping – a simple throw away comment, or an ill-conceived status update.

I briefed my friends on what was really going on, set up a fake profile and changed my relationship status: Mark is now in a relationship with Colin. I had a friend primed to comment for me: 'It's about time you told people – I'm so happy for you.' And I left it on my profile for all of five minutes.

We'll never know which family member saw it, or who was the one to pass the info on to the rest of the family. But I underestimated my family. There's a lot of very religious people in my family, including a couple of baptist preachers. And although nobody said a single word to me, they obviously weighed in with one another because a week later, I got another letter.

Dear Mark, while we respect your right to live your own life, we cannot agree with your current lifestyle choice, you will not be welcome at the upcoming family wedding. We would prefer it if you did not attend.

Unsigned.

Darlington, 11th July 2011

Losers

By Mark McKnight

Who would be a teenager again? Certainly not me! Even if you paid me. Primary School was a fairly unpleasant experience. I was an awkward middle child. Looking back, I don't really know why I didn't develop the social skills to make me one of the popular kids. A twist of fate? A mistake on the part of my parents? I guess we'll never know. I couldn't wait to leave primary school behind me. Leave my reputation behind as the kid who picked his nose. And worse still, the vicar's son.

High school wasn't really that much better. It was bigger. I was more anonymous. But the awkward kid had turned into an awkward teenager. And the gap between rich and poor, between the popular kids and the outsiders like me just got wider and wider. Of course, there were the jocks. And the fundamental Christians. Then there were the drama kids, the party animals and the music club. Unfortunately, I never quite found my feet in any of the cliques. So I and half a dozen other 'losers' formed our own little clique. The 'don't quite fit in anywhere else' clique.

So although the rest of my peers were (I assume) courting and shifting to their heart's content, despite our best efforts, there was a significant lack of any real boy/girl action in the loser camp. At sixteen, there was a moment of hope when Tim, another vicar's son, found himself a girlfriend. (That girlfriend has turned into a beautiful woman, and they're now married with four kids). However, none of the rest of us seemed to have any luck with the ladies.

We've all lost contact. I wonder what happened to the rest of the losers. Last I heard, one of them was an accountant working for one of the big five. Another had been suspended from his computer science course on suspicion of hacking computers. A third became a vicar himself (the aforementioned Tim), before he was summarily defrocked for financial irregularities. Three more are missing in action. They never popped up on Facebook. We can only assume they are dead or else working for intelligence services.

Fourteen years later, I'm fairing reasonably in my career. I love my job, I'm earning great money and have as much job security as there is in this day and age. I have a good bunch of friends around me. Life is good. But still no ring on my finger. Still no real success with the ladies.

But there's this great girl behind the counter in a smoothie shop that I go to. I mostly go there to flirt with her, so I'm in at least once a day. The smoothies are great, but that's just a bonus. For once in my life, there's a chance that I might actually be having some luck with the ladies, so to speak. And I'm terrified that I'm going to screw it up and that she'll find out that I'm one of the losers.

Darlington, 14th July 2011

Emily Williams Posted On Your Wall

By Mark McKnight

 :)

 :)

 Hello you!

 Irish man!

 Lol! English lady! :)

 WUU2?

 Getting my Dumbledore costume ready :)

 Dumbledore? I had no idea you were so cool!

 Lol! Believe it! Two day long Harry Potter party!!!!

 Irish man!

 Go away Darren, he was my friend first! Get your own!.....Loser!

 Snort....

 Wow! It's a proper smoothie turf war!
PS English man!

 Stay out of this Irish man, this is between me and Darren. Whoever wins, claims you. You don't get any say! x

 Erm...You can have him. I'm a married man! ;)

 The sweet smell of victory! Loser!
I just ready your 'talent'......hahahahahaha! Amazing!
x

 :) I have hidden depths! x

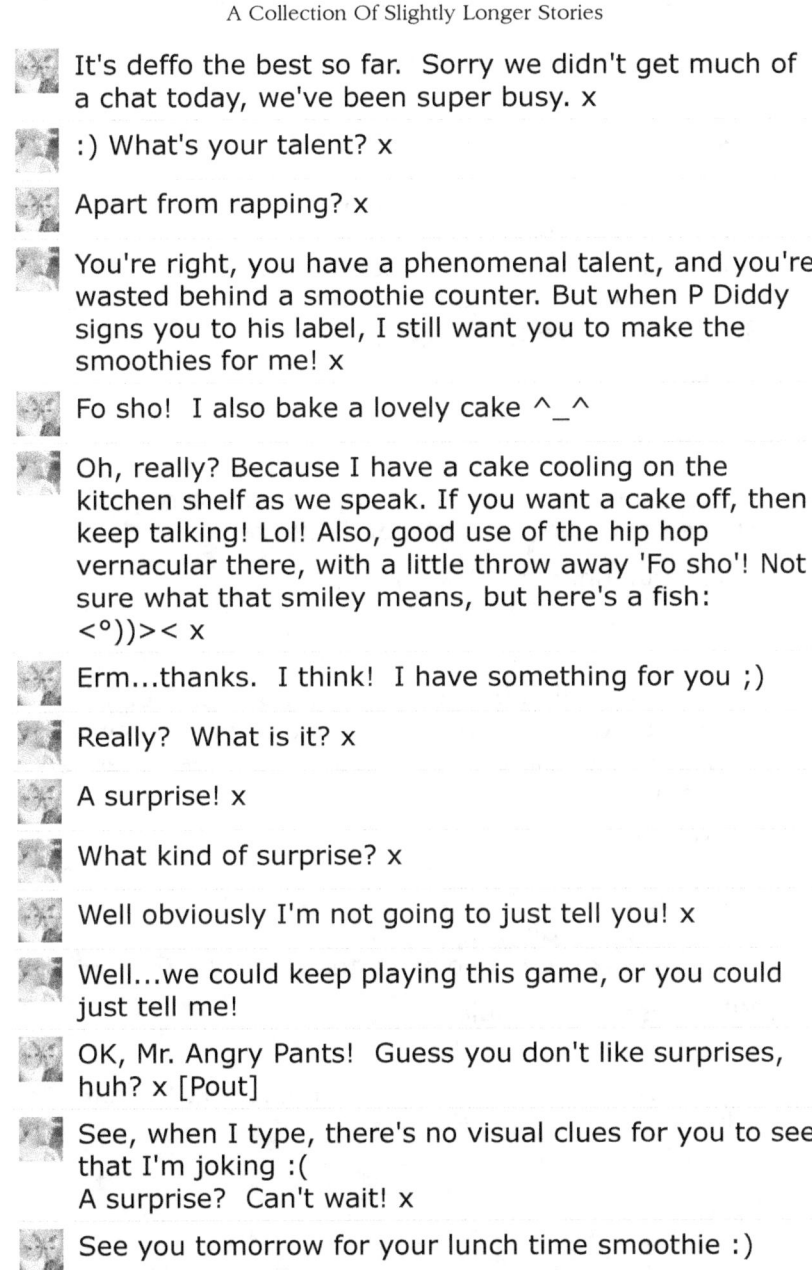

It's deffo the best so far. Sorry we didn't get much of a chat today, we've been super busy. x

:) What's your talent? x

Apart from rapping? x

You're right, you have a phenomenal talent, and you're wasted behind a smoothie counter. But when P Diddy signs you to his label, I still want you to make the smoothies for me! x

Fo sho! I also bake a lovely cake ^_^

Oh, really? Because I have a cake cooling on the kitchen shelf as we speak. If you want a cake off, then keep talking! Lol! Also, good use of the hip hop vernacular there, with a little throw away 'Fo sho'! Not sure what that smiley means, but here's a fish: <°))>< x

Erm...thanks. I think! I have something for you ;)

Really? What is it? x

A surprise! x

What kind of surprise? x

Well obviously I'm not going to just tell you! x

Well...we could keep playing this game, or you could just tell me!

OK, Mr. Angry Pants! Guess you don't like surprises, huh? x [Pout]

See, when I type, there's no visual clues for you to see that I'm joking :(
A surprise? Can't wait! x

See you tomorrow for your lunch time smoothie :)

:) Why, yes. Yes you will! x

Loyalty cards? I love it! Even more reasons for me to buy smoothies! x

Even more reasons? x

Yes. Reasons to drink smoothies:
They're awesome
The people behind the counter are awesome
Loyalty cards. Only four more until I get a free one!
To clarify: a free smoothie ;)

[Blush] Thanks! x

You're welcome :) x

AND, I have even more exciting news...we're going to [fingers crossed] start smoothie deliveries!

Oh zohhhhhhhhhhhh!!!!!!!!

?

dm! That would qualify as reason number four! :)
What, so I'd just phone up and you'd come running?
That way, I would own you, rather than the other way around!

Ha Ha!!!!

Sooooooo...
...I was wondering....
...if you'd like to get some coffee some time?

Why, yes! Yes I would! x

Darlington, 14th July 2011

Lottery

By Mark McKnight

A hundred and sixty six million pounds. That's the jackpot for tonight's lottery. A fourteen times rollover. What would you do with the money? Of course, I would give most of it away. Do a bit of good here and there. Donate a bunch to causes that I really believe in. Lavish it on the people that I love and care about. Of course, I'd keep a bit for myself. Maybe a million or two. Even at three percent, I could live off the interest quite comfortably. On a million, I'd be earning thirty grand a year.

It's easy to make jokes about the money when you haven't won it yet. In the newsagents where I bought my ticket, I was happy to make some wisecracks with the lass behind the counter and a couple of other customers. To joke around about who was going to win. About how we'd happily share it between two of us but not between three. I went for a lucky dip – after all, one set of numbers has no more kismet attached to it than another.

When I buy a lottery ticket, it's with only an outside's hope – not honestly expecting to win anything. My absolute best hope would be to match a couple of numbers and win a couple of quid. I more or less forgot about it for the rest of the day and most of the next day too. But when I got home from work, I fired the app up on my phone to check the results. Hmmm...those numbers seemed awfully familiar. Where was my ticket?

I eventually found my ticket and checked the numbers...1...2...3...4...5. And both bonus numbers too. Check again...it's legit! Matched all seven numbers!

What do I do now? I just not sure....

Read the rules on the back of the ticket. Phone the number. It's a bona fide claim. What now? What now? What now?

The lady on the claim line gives me a couple of pieces of advice: only tell close friends and family and stay away from the media until you have someone to advise you. They are sending someone straight away – he'll be with me in under an hour.

Phone my mam, my best friend and my girlfriend. Oh, wait! I don't have a girlfriend. Perhaps now that I have money, that might change!

Long story short: new house, new town, new friends, new girlfriend. Of course, the old guard are never too keen on 'new' money. I'd love to be able to do more with the hundred and fifty million I have left, but it's all tied up in medium and long term investments. But it's not like home. I had good friends back then who didn't care how much my stock portfolio was worth – only if I was buying a round. I was single, but I wasn't fretting about gold diggers. I didn't have to deal with a sack load of begging letters every day the postman delivered.

Darlington, 14th July 2011

Best Man

By Mark McKnight

Welcome, boys, girls, ladies and gentlemen, to the wedding of the century. This is truly a day that we have all looked forward to with bated breath. Of course, I'm clearly not the best man – if I was the best man, I would be the one getting married today [pause for laughter]. But it's an honour nonetheless to be invited to this beautiful venue, in this beautiful city, with these beautiful bridesmaids [wink and raise glass].

No [pause] more [pause] secrets.

So, Adam and Jenny. Actually, words can't express what I feel about these two beautiful people. So I've decided to communicate to you today through the medium of interpretive dance! [Cue track: This Is Why I'm Hot. Finish dance by kissing Adam on the head]

It's the traditional job of the best man to poke a little bit of fun at the groom. The only problem was, I realised that most of the stories that incriminate Adam portray me in a worse light. So I'm not going to tell you about the night we accidentally spent the night at a brothel. Or the time we were threatened with a shotgun in a road rage incident.

I will tell you one story though. Once, when we were living in Africa, we were lying on our bunks chatting about running with the bulls. For those of you who don't know, in Pamplona in Spain, it's traditional for men to run ahead of a dozen bulls as they make their way to the bullfighting ring. Needless to say, it's a dangerous enough activity. It was right after Adam and Jenny had started dating. I asked Adam if he'd ever run with the bulls. "No way," he answered. "I have too much to live for." [Pause for awwwww...]

When Adam first started dating Jenny, none of us had met her. We were all far, far away. So when he told us he' had found a girlfriend and she was this hot blond, we thought he was making it all up. Then when he sent us a picture, we thought he had cut it out of a magazine or something! But as it turns out, and I'm sure you'll all agree, she really is as beautiful as Adam led us all to believe. So before I go on, let me toast the bride. To Jenny! [Toast with champagne].

So just like Adam sang to Jenny during the ceremony, I'd like to sing to you too. I'm sure lots of you know it – from the Lion King. Please feel free to sing along. Here goes...[Waste plenty of time preparing to sing]

Nants ingonyama bagithi Baba
Sithi uhm ingonyama
[Pause for laughter]
Let me finish with an Irish blessing:
May the road rise up to meet you.
May the wind always be at your back.
May the sun shine warm upon your face,
and rains fall soft upon your fields.
And until we meet again,
May God hold you in the palm of His hand.

Darlington, 14th July 2011

Things I Have Done To Impress A Girl

By Mark McKnight

Things I have done to impress a girl:
1. I became a vegetarian
2. For a different girl, I tried to eat a two pound steak. I failed!
3. I became an activist
   - And in so doing, I lived on a protest site for three whole days
   - Then I thought about growing my hair long but instead grew my beard long
   - I pretended to care about climate change.
   - I pretended to care about animal rights.
   - I pretended to care about the arms trade.
   - Then I discovered I actually did care about all those things.
4. I became a vegan. Then I realised that although she was completely hot, being a vegan was just too hard!
5. I spent a bunch of money that I didn't have on a car that I thought would impress her. She was impressed by the car, but then less than impressed at how I wasn't able to take her out anywhere because I was so broke!
6. I bought a blue satin shirt that became known as my 'pulling shirt'. I only had the guts to wear it out twice and it had a one hundred percent hit rate. But there's a big responsibility in owning a shirt like that.
7. I danced with a girl on an empty dance floor, even though all my friends were watching. I hate dancing! It's not that I don't want to, it's just that often when I do, people laugh at me. But she wanted to. So I did.
8. I pretended I liked her pets
   - One girl had a bunch of guinea pigs. She even made a birthday cake for them. And so I said the word "Awwwww..." when it was appropriate.
   - Another girl was into her cats. I used to kick them when no-one was watching so that they'd stay away from me.
   - Snakes. Enough said!
9. I lost thirty pounds. That wasn't for a specific girl. More to make me more appealing to all girls. Has it worked? Time will tell!

10. I learned how to play the guitar. And then learned how to sing. And then wrote a song about how my love for her would never change. That I'd always be there and always care. Then I moved away, didn't see her for ten years and blurted out that I still have feelings for her. But she didn't have feelings for me any more.

11. Art galleries, museum openings, weddings of people that I don't know, home furnishings, paint shopping!

12. And then there's the futile efforts on Valentine's Day over the years: chocolates in heart shaped boxes, dozens of red roses (both real and artificial, depending on my financial fortunes), cards, gifts and all manner of plush toys.

13. And probably worst of all, on more than one occasion I drank way too much and then
    - Thought I could dance
    - Thought I was funny
    - Thought she was flirting with me

Darlington, 26th July 2011

Lifelong Ambition

By Mark McKnight

Today I fulfilled one of my actual lifelong ambitions. I played sax with the Alf Hinds Big Band. And words simply cannot express how much I enjoyed the experience. Even now, almost an hour later I'm properly buzzing.

I had fairly mediocre career as a musician back in the day. I was a talented flute player amongst a peer group of flautist demi gods. Like a coterie made up entirely of Pan himself. I did the run round the local youth orchestras and wind bands. I rose to the dizzying heights of principal flute for the Belfast Youth Orchestra and even toured America briefly. But my assistant principal and I had a deal – I would play all the solos and she would play all the difficult bits. It worked quite nicely!

One day I was chatting to a friend who offered me work on the saxophone. The money was too good to turn down so I borrowed an instrument and learned how to play. (The very same instrument that I was playing on tonight). And that was when my musical career took an unexpected turn for the better.

The North Irish Territorial Army Band was the paid work. There I was on 2nd Tenor and Baritone Sax when the need arose. It was the easiest money I've ever earned. They used to say we were one of the best bands in the British Army with some of the worst military skills.

P-Jazz was a different outfit entirely. A two piece jazz ensemble, we were once described as fantastic porno-jazz. Hence the name.

I also played in a band called White Saturday. It sort of sat awkwardly between a lot of genres – soul, funk, jazz, hip hop... Our drummer would only rehearse if we brought him pistachios. We eventually broke up because of a fight (actual punches thrown) between the guitarist and bassist.

Of course, I've played in plenty of worship bands over the years of varying quality but have never quite been convinced of the value of a melody instrument in worship. I did enjoy being a part of the whole 'tower of power' experience, though.

Then a couple of weeks ago, I was telling my friend that I'd always wanted to play in a big band. And he said, "I might know a big band that's looking for a saxophone." And that brings you up to speed.

It was everything I had hope it would be – just sitting in on a rehearsal was immensely satisfying. Pulling out old jazz standards like 'Makin' Whoopee' and 'That Ole Devil Called Love.' Of course, if we ever play 'Sing, Sing, Sing' by Benny Goodman, I may actually pee my pants with excitement!

Fulfilling your lifelong ambitions is something that I can wholeheartedly recommend. It wasn't something enormous. It wasn't earth shattering. But it was something that was important to me – I'd always wanted to do it, and there's an open invitation for me to continue to sit in.

Darlington, 5th September 2011

Silence

By Mark McKnight

Silence. It's often a beautiful thing. A place to find yourself. Or connect with your god. Or to just stop and relax.

But this silence is tearing me up.

Let me rewind a bit. I met a girl this weekend. An attractively spiritual, stunningly beautiful, humbly challenging, bewitchingly vulnerable girl. Uncharacteristically, I went right up to her and her friend in a bar and started talking to them. Twice we got kicked out because they wanted to close the bar. We salsa danced together. We held our cider in the air and sang hymns at the top of our lungs. We danced on tables in the pub.

We even managed what in anyone else's life would be called a date – I drove an hour and a half in the wrong direction just so we could have lunch together. If I wasn't such a nice guy, I'd have tried some moves on. Damn my good nature and integrity! But I genuinely enjoyed myself. I thought there was chemistry and was happy to hang out until she's over her last boyf.

But this lovely Welsh girl has messed me up more than I quite understand yet. This is me we're talking about. I'm solid. Dependable. Happy-go-lucky. Unphased by the fickle arrows from Cupid's bow. A rock in a troubled sea. Yet somehow this girl has found some kind of chink in my armour and totally screwed me up for the last week. This is uncharted territory for me. Usually I'm quite adept at using the words 'It's all good' like a blanket that I can throw over things that I don't want to think about or that I can do nothing about.

The problem is that since we had lunch together a week ago, there has been a single missive from her: "Glad u got there safely. Thanku for brunch :D x"

This is the silence that is tearing me apart. Why my head is such a mess. Why all my insecurities are coming flooding in. Why the confidence (real or fake) to make me walk straight up to her at the bar is all fading away into 'Why would she be interested in a guy like me?'

If she weren't interested, I would be cool with that. I'd be gutted, but there would be nothing I could do. Chalk another one up to experience. If she was interested but now isn't the right time, I would be cool with that. I can play a long game. I can wait. Work out how I can make it work. If she got back with the old boyfriend, I probably wouldn't be cool with that. But again, 'it's all good.' Nothing I could do about it.

But for now, I just don't know the truth. She's ignoring my texts. I don't have the guts to call her. What can I do? Listen to meaningless platitudes from idiot friends? And continue shouting at God in the hopes that this will finally be the one.

Darlington, 5th September 2011

Home 2

By Mark McKnight

"Are you not nearly thinking about moving back home?"
That seems to be the growing cry from my nearest and dearest
back in Belfast. What is there for me back there?

Three hundred years of hatred don't go away overnight.
The war continues. Don't be fooled – there's still plenty of people
consumed by their hate. Even though they're not fighting, they're
planning. The ballot box and the armalite.

And what about all my people? A brother who doesn't
speak to me. My mam. A few cousins who mostly aren't
interested. Of course, there's some friends from back in the day
who I still look up when I'm back there. But not one has made the
effort to call me. Not one single friend has come to Darlington to
visit. They want me to come back, but in the last 10 years it's
been all me – I've phoned, I've emailed, I've made the effort to see
what's happening in their lives.

It's a curse that everyone who has travelled faces when
they come back. A wise man once said that when you travel, you
never come all the way home. For a while, I thought home was
Northern Ireland. Then I thought it was Uganda. Somehow I
ended up making a home and setting down some roots with the
infidel English.

But just when you think you're comfortable, all kinds of
things start falling apart on you. You realise that your next step
could commit you to moving house every 5 years (or less) for the
rest of your life. And you meet a pretty girl that lives nearly 300
miles away. And both your house mates decide that it's time to
move on leaving you with a messy house and a £400 pay cut.

All of a sudden, the solid ground of home that was just
under your feet starts to get a bit like quicksand. And the first
thing you want to do is escape. You look for things that mean you
don't have to be home alone any more – join a jazz band, take up
salsa dancing and the like.

The truth, however, is that when you're by yourself a
home is just somewhere to sleep and store your stuff. There's no
sentimental reason to hurry home from work. Early to bed, early
to rise is meaningless. Why would you get up early to a cold,
empty house?

For me, a home is about the people. I'm blessed to live in
this stupidly big four bedroom house where I don't know what to
do with all the space. When I moved in, people said I should fill it

up with a wife and kids! But here I am, alone in this huge space.

I would trade it in a heartbeat for a bedsit with someone that I want to spend the rest of my life with. Because that would be the home that I'm only just realising that I've been yearning for all these years.

Darlington, 6th September 2011

Emotional Vacuum

By Mark McKnight

I've always been up front and honest about it – I haven't cried since 1996. I remember it clearly – I was getting ready to go on stage to perform in the chorus line of Grease. Word got passed on to me that my grandma had passed away during the afternoon. I found a quiet place, shed a few tears, got myself back together and then went on stage.

There's no real reason for me having stopped crying at that stage. It just kind of happened. I just haven't really felt the need ever since to shed any tears. Fifteen years is probably too long not to cry. I'm worried that some day all those years of bottling it up will come out at once. I'll be a wreck for days, unable to stop crying.

It's true, I've had the accusation of 'emotional vacuum' levelled towards me on more than one occasion. And for a long time, I though that was reasonably true. I mean, quantity and quality of tears are usually a fairly good indicator of emotional depth.

But it turns out that I've been misled on this whole issue. For most of my life, I assumed that because I'm a guy expression of feelings was not only difficult, but maybe even genetically impossible! And then I meet this amazing girl. Suddenly, all I want to do is talk about my feelings. And what surprises me even more is that there are all kinds of weird feelings in there that I can't even vocalise, never mind understand.

Even more than that, when I look at some of my mates, they're even worse at expressing their feelings than I am. Like some friends who have been in love for the last ten years (no word of a lie) and never quite gotten it together because neither one of them can say how they feel. Or my friend who's about to leave for uni and her dad is desperately trying to reach out and connect with her but doesn't know how so they just end up arguing. And she can't even give him a hug and tell him she loves him.

So even though I have this whole raft of new emotions that I don't quite know what to do with, I at least have tried to articulate them, both to this lovely young Welsh lady and to my friends who mostly think I'm mental because this is a side of Marko that they haven't ever seen.

The interesting thing about my whole emotional reawakening is that there haven't been any tears involved to date. None. Nada. Zip. Zilch. Perhaps they are yet to come.

Because, sadly, at the moment, things aren't going so well with the lovely young Welsh lady. I haven't heard or seen hide nor hair of her in over a week. I'm concerned that all too soon I'm going to have to accept defeat and then, perhaps, after fifteen years, the waterworks may well be back in business.

Darlington, 6th September 2011

If...

By Mark McKnight

If my dad hadn't had an affair, my parents would never have separated. If my parents hadn't separated, I would never have moved back into town and changed churches. If I hadn't changed church, I would never have joined the youth group and become a Christian. If I hadn't become a Christian, I would never have played in the worship group growing up. If I hadn't played in the worship group, I would never have studied music at uni. If I hadn't studied music, I would never have lived in the Church of Ireland centre. If I hadn't lived in the Church of Ireland centre, I would never have led worship there. If I hadn't led worship at the Church of the Res, I would never have recorded my own album, conceived Christmas Unwrapped and started a gospel choir. If I hadn't started my own gospel choir, I would never have got the job working for the African Children's Choir and toured the world. If I hadn't got the job as musical supervisor (such as it was), I would never have gone to Africa. If I hadn't gone to Africa, I would have drifted into obscurity in Belfast, probably marrying some nice teacher and missing out on all that God had for me later. If I hadn't gone to Africa, I would never have met James and ended up working for Mwangaza. If I hadn't worked for Mwangaza, I would never have ended up back in Uganda doing all kinds of crazy stuff that I never even dreamed of – farm manager, children's home manager, audio & video consultant. If I hadn't gone back to Uganda, I would never had to endure the stress of that mission trip that almost tore me apart. I never had to endure the stress, I wouldn't have seen Adam fall in love and marry his perfect woman. If I hadn't seen Adam fall in love, I would never have known what I was missing out on. If I hadn't know what I was missing out on, the last five years would have been a whole lot easier on me. If I hadn't endured the stress of Africa, I would never have come back to England and gone to work in Harrogate. If I hadn't messed up so much in Harrogate, my life wouldn't have fallen apart. If my life hadn't disintegrated, I would never have had to rely so much on MLS to survive. If I hadn't had to rely on MLS so much, I would never have worked for Just 10. If I hadn't worked for Just 10, I would never have ended up in Darlington. If I hadn't gotten to Darlington, I would never have gone to Greenbelt. If I hadn't gotten so fixated with Greenbelt, I wouldn't have met you. And if I hadn't met you a fortnight ago, I wouldn't be hurting so much right now. And if I wasn't hurting so much, there would be no such thing as hope...

Darlington, 10th September 2011

Rock Music

By Mark McKnight

So I was driving home today and flicking through the CDs in my 6 disc multi changer (oh yes, that's how middle class I am). Then it occurs to me that I'm listening to a whole lot of fairly emo music at the moment. I mean, not proper slit your wrists stuff, just a lot of fairly emotional stuff that I imagine 'diet-emos' listen to. Activist singer songwriters who croon about war and love and hummingbirds and songs in Portuguese that I don't understand.

On the way home, I decided to do something about it – my playlists are getting a bit stale and it's time to reconnect with my roots. Like most teenage boys, I went through a hard rock phase. Angry, screaming vocals. Wailing guitars solos that could melt your face. Drum riffs that could cut a man in half from fifty yards. Haircuts that defy both belief and gravity. And more male exposed flesh than most pubescent boys are entirely comfortable with.

Somehow I never quite made the jump to heavy metal. It just all seemed a bit too screamo for me. Little did I realise the subtle distinctions – punk, metal and such like. For of late, I've strayed down something of a gypsy punk line which in retrospect seems like an obvious next step after a teen hard rock phase. I digress. While my brother and his peers went further down the road of Metallica and towards Scumdogs of the Universe, I was happy to stick with Guns 'n' Roses and Motley Crue.

But a passionate devotee I remained of hard rock. Able to quote lyrics and defend my own swearing because I was hearing it in songs on a semi regular basis. I even learned a few chords on an old acoustic guitar and learned some of their more playable numbers. I tried to impress a few girls with them, but we all know that if you're trying to woo the ladies, you need to stick with Simon and/or Garfunkel.

To my horror, when I dug out my old cassettes and LPs (let's face it, I bought some tracks on iTunes), I discovered that the hard rock foundation that my teen years had been built on was a sham. I idled through bits of songs I used to love. Songs with angry lyrics that captured the teenage angst of 1995 in a way that nothing else could. And they just don't do it for me any more.

And to my shame, I find myself listening to Gladys Knight and the Pips. And then some Aretha. I don't have any deep and philosophical insight as to why that is – I'd just rather listen to music that I can tap my foot to and that uplifts my soul. I was an angry young man once, confused and painfully shy. Angry rock music spoke to me once upon a time.

Just don't tell my mam, because loud rock music is a great way to wind her up!

Darlington, 10th September 2011

Lonely

By Mark McKnight

I thought I was independent. I thought I was unshakeable.
I thought I could get through life by myself, drift on without
needing anyone else to make me complete. I was selfish and
alone.

Lately, it's occurred to me that being by myself isn't as
much fun as it used to be. Young Jonno moved on last weekend
and Philippe has fixed his move date for this weekend. Standing
in Jon's empty room, it occurs to me the implications of the
decisions that others have made. For the first time in over three
years, I'm about to rattle around my four bedroom house all alone.
I can create my own little world of music and art and storytelling
and creativity. I can close a door and no-one else has the right to
open it. And there was a time when that was all I wanted – a
space of my own where nobody could invade. Not Rashid. Not
Kigozi. Not Bamwenda. Not Shifah. Not Swabra. Not even
Adam or James.

But there's something different this time. Shutting
everyone else out does something worse. It shuts me in. Selfish
and alone. A key is a mystical thing, filled with promise and
potential. To hold a key is to hold power. But to hold the only
key is a heavy weight.

Sometimes, I come home at the end of a tiring day and
ironically call out, "Honey, I'm home!" And the silence screams
back at me. Bringing all the insecurities and fears of being alone
rushing down the stairs – like the opposite of a daughter jumping
into her daddy's arms and sitting on his lap to tell him about the
day.

Every night I get into bed, crushed yet again by the
gnawing emptiness of yet another repose in my single bed. I have
the money – I'd splash out on a double, but what's the point?

Sometimes, when I'm feeling up to it, I'll cook a meal. For
one. I don't get cooking. I love taking care of people I love. So
cooking for family and friends is no effort. But when it's just me,
I'm not bothered. So cooking means throwing something from the
freezer into the oven. For one. And I switch the television on, not
because there's anything worth watching, but for company. To
hear human voices and laugh at their jokes. To be a part of a
group, rather than to live in isolation – selfish and alone.

What's the solution? Is there a solution? It's a vicious
circle. Loneliness makes me maudlin. And the foolish

sentimentality makes me want to shut the door, not open it up. Mawkishness is a very unattractive quality by any standard. I really don't know or understand how life reached this place. Every girl that comes along is unattractive, unavailable or unhinged. And the advice that comes from friends is so piss-poor as to make me seriously think about unfriending them both on the social networks and in real life.

Darlington, 28th September 2011

Hope

By Mark McKnight

Hope.

What exactly is it? Who invented it? What's it for? How do you find it? How do you lose it?

And the most important question of all: why on earth do friends seem to unanimously miss the point of hope when all you need is someone to be a rock. Someone to say, "You know what, a higher power has this under control. You don't need to worry. This is already sorted. It's already been taken care of. And just in case you missed it the first time, you don't need to worry!"

But instead, when all you want is the tiniest glimmer of hope, the best that almost everyone can put up is an unpleasant dose of realism. "Well, maybe it's time to move on. At least you'll have learned XYZ for next time. It's good that you've learned so much about yourself through all this. Maybe what you've learned this time will help you next time. You should be encouraged that you had the courage to do such and such. Even though it didn't work out the way you expected, you can at least take heart in that."

Of course, all this advice comes from a good place - they want to see you happy. Friends don't want to see each other hurt or in pain. So they call it as they see it. So in as gentle a manner as they can muster, they try to convince you that there is no hope and that it's time to move on. Of course, they might not even realise they're doing it - it's probably a sub-conscious reaction. Nobody wants to move on. Or listen to the voice of reason. When it's something that we really want, we will hold on to the tiniest glimmer of hope, however small. And all we want is for the people we love and care about to tell us, "You know what, a higher power has this under control. You don't need to worry. This is already sorted. It's already been taken care of. And just in case you missed it the first time, you don't need to worry!"

But nobody does. They don't hear the words they say and don't realise the pain they cause. In trying to protect you, they end up completely missing the point of what you want from them.

Hope is a fickle thing. One day strong and healthy, the next sickly and weak. It's hard to keep hope when you're the only one. When you're the only one who doesn't want to let it go. When you're the only one who has the whisper inside your head, 'I know what the facts are, but that doesn't mean all is lost. It just means I need to hold on a bit longer.'

Hope means that in spite of overwhelming evidence to the contrary, and friends who just want to stop you getting hurt, that you're not ready to give up. When one in a million seems like good odds.

Darlington, 28th September 2011

Power

By Mark McKnight

Everybody seems to be telling me how great a job I'm doing these days. There was a mention in our church magazine: **"COMMENTS HAVE BEEN RECEIVED REGARDING MARK MCKNIGHT!!** And these culminate in the pleasant requirement to say a BIG THANK YOU TO MARK for the two wonderful services he has recently held on Sunday mornings – the music and worship was uplifting to many and thoroughly enjoyed. It was good to see so many of the uniformed youth and their parents at the Parade service."

The schools I go into think I'm great, even though I've actually cut back the amount of stuff that I do for them – the head teachers especially have been raving about how great the work that I do is.

My boss was in a funeral director's office the other day. Even she was singing my praises, even though she has neither met nor spoken to me. The grumpy old ladies in church (Scary Mary and Mean Jean) have even been won over and for the first time ever came up to my face and genuinely complimented me on some of the good stuff that's happening.

Now I don't say all this to be conceited in a, 'Look at me, aren't I great' way. The truth is, I'm a little bit embarrassed by it all. Because in my mind, it's great that some stuff is working. But there's a bunch of stuff that isn't really working. A load of things that I feel like I can't give the attention they deserve. And a desk full of things that really should be done but when it comes down to the wire, probably never will be dealt with.

But worse than all that is the vain temptation of pride and power. I see others (who I place in the 'idiot' category) doing great things. Their ministry seems to increase in size and influence. They are loved by the hoi polloi, courted by the important and given an open door to the vacuous world of Christian super stardom.

And the question begins to gnaw, 'If my ministry is so great, how come people don't know who I am? How come I'm not important? How come I'm not famous?' I'm ambitious – I want to do things bigger and better. I want to see more kids at my groups. I want my ministry to be popular and effective and growing and innovative. And as much as I want all those things, I want to be recognised for it. I want people to ask me for advice. I want to be the one asked to go places to speak.

I know it's not right – I know I should be happy where God has put me. I should be comfortable in the knowledge that I'm doing God's work here in the Costa Del Darlo. But I'm human, and I know that it is a daily battle to maintain my integrity and to faithfully minister this furrow. Maybe for now?

Darlington, 29th September 2011

The Meeting

By Mark McKnight

This afternoon, I was sitting in a meeting and only partly paying attention. I'll be honest, one of the advantages of taking an iPad into meetings with you is that when things get boring, you can go onto Twitter or see what's happening on Facebook.

About half way through the meeting, somebody sprung something on me that I really wasn't expecting. Someone said, "Listen up, Mark!" and then they proceeded to lay out their great plan. Now I'm not naïve enough to think that their idea isn't without value. It actually might make a lot of sense if I was planning on being around town for an awful lot longer.

The short version is that I get a house with my job. They have another house that's empty which costs less to maintain than mine does. But it's way across town and I have no real desire to move house anyway. The problem is that it weighs my own personal preference and comfort against the financial and organisational preferences and comfort of everyone else.

It's not the first time that I've heard the idea, but it's the first time it's reached me through official channels. Yet instead of taking me out for coffee to sound me out about it, to have a quiet word so to speak, it was trumped as this fantastic new idea in the midst of a staff meeting with our entire team listening.

I'm just angry at the way they went about the whole thing – neither of my bosses knew that this was coming up at the meeting. Nobody had briefed them in advance. It was thrust forward as this idea that was going to solve everyone's problems, including mine.

Of course, it is possible that I've become too comfortable. I've been here for more than 3 years now, and have gathered enough moss to make moving house a significant issue. It's as much about not wanting to deal with the messiness of moving and the hassle of having to pack everything to move about a mile and a half as anything else. I can dress it all up in excuses about ministry and being rooted in community. The truth is, I just don't want to move.

But then what of the simple life to which I have so desperately clung to in the past? Tried and tried to keep to a life free from complication? And now I have art on my walls. I use a filing cabinet. Things have a 'place' where they belong. Is this a good thing? Or a bad thing? Or a foolish thing?

Time alone will tell how long I remain here. I seem to

have unwittingly fallen in love. Maybe I'll be moving sooner than I thought. Maybe my world will implode because it's unrequited. Maybe for the first time in a long time, my feet are starting to get a little bit itchy again? This is just a house, daily seeming less and less like a home.

Darlington, 12th – 29th September 2011